LOVERS OF JANINE

Janine is a professional dancer — admired, adored, envied. Her life in Monte Carlo should be glamourous and exciting, but she is desperately unhappy. She suspects her lover, the fascinating Nikko, of cheating on her with rich society women. Nevertheless, her infatuation with him makes her an easy pawn in his ambitious and selfish game — a game that involves deceit, blackmail, and murder; and which drives Janine into two marriages and almost destroys her relationship with the passionate and devoted Peter Willington.

Books by Denise Robins
in the Linford Romance Library:

GYPSY LOVER
KISS OF YOUTH
THE ENDURING FLAME
FAMILY HOLIDAY
BRIEF ECSTASY
THE TIGER IN MEN
LIGHT THE CANDLES
THE PRICE OF FOLLY
THE BOUNDARY LINE
TWO LOVES

SPECIAL MESSAGE TO READERS

THE ULVERSCROFT FOUNDATION
(registered UK charity number 264873)
was established in 1972 to provide funds for research, diagnosis and treatment of eye diseases. Examples of major projects funded by the Ulverscroft Foundation are:-

- The Children's Eye Unit at Moorfields Eye Hospital, London
- The Ulverscroft Children's Eye Unit at Great Ormond Street Hospital for Sick Children
- Funding research into eye diseases and treatment at the Department of Ophthalmology, University of Leicester
- The Ulverscroft Vision Research Group, Institute of Child Health
- Twin operating theatres at the Western Ophthalmic Hospital, London
- The Chair of Ophthalmology at the Royal Australian College of Ophthalmologists

You can help further the work of the Foundation by making a donation or leaving a legacy. Every contribution is gratefully received. If you would like to help support the Foundation or require further information, please contact:

THE ULVERSCROFT FOUNDATION
The Green, Bradgate Road, Anstey
Leicester LE7 7FU, England
Tel: (0116) 236 4325

website: www.foundation.ulverscroft.com

DENISE ROBINS

LOVERS OF JANINE

Complete and Unabridged

LINFORD
Leicester

First published in Great Britain in 1931

First Linford Edition
published 2019

A catalogue record for this book is available from the British Library.

ISBN 978–1–4448–3970–8

Published by
F. A. Thorpe (Publishing)
Anstey, Leicestershire

Set by Words & Graphics Ltd.
Anstey, Leicestershire
Printed and bound in Great Britain by
T. J. International Ltd., Padstow, Cornwall

This book is printed on acid-free paper

1

The orchestra stopped playing. The dancers on the smooth shining floor of the Palm Court in the Hotel d'Etoile stood still and looked at the leader of the band which had been playing so gaily. He was about to make an announcement — fiddle under his arm — hand upraised. He was an American and spoke in his native tongue. But the Etoile was French and one of the newest and most fashionable hotels in Monte Carlo. A cosmopolitan crowd — men and women of every nation — gathered here for a few weeks' hectic pleasure. Most of them understood the American who conducted his jazz band so excellently.

'Ladies and gentlemen! We are now going to ask you to take your seats for the Exhibition dance. I wanna introduce to you that wonnerful lady you already know — Janine — the loveliest dancer in Europe, and her wonnerful partner, Nikko!'

The drum rolled. Saxophones blared. A spotlight flung a glittering circle on to the floor and everywhere else the lights mysteriously faded out. Into that all-revealing circle stepped a man and a girl, hand in hand. They smiled and bowed as an enthusiastic burst of applause greeted them.

The men in the room focused eager glances on Janine. The 'loveliest dancer in Europe', the conductor of the orchestra had called her. And rightly. Not a male heart but quickened at the sight of her loveliness; a figure of alluring grace in the long billowing dress of white tulle, which swept to the tiny feet in jade-green shoes with high, jewelled heels. Her throat and shoulders and arms seemed no whiter than the dress. Emeralds — who was to know whether real or fake — were wound about the slender neck. Bracelets, a dozen, or more, sparkled half-way up one exquisite arm. The cruel revealing blaze of arc-light could not find defect in the charming face. The wide eyes were more green than blue under heavy black lashes; the mouth, a perfect curve, with short, passionate upper-lip. The tip-tilted nose gave the whole face an air of charming youthfulness. Janine had a shining head of pale gold hair pinned into a knot at the nape of her neck and showing small ears in which two drop diamonds flashed and twinkled as she moved her head.

If the men in the Palm Court concentrated upon the girl, a great many feminine eyes turned to her partner, Nikko. He was the rage in Monte Carlo. Women — French, English, American — flocked to the Hotel d'Etoile to see him — to have him for an hour's instruction. Handsome, fascinating Nikko, with his lithe figure, graceful as a panther's; his dark head with blue-black hair.

He was an artist to his finger-tips — both as a dancer and a lover. And if he left a trail of wounded pride, of hurt love, of agonizing jealousy behind him — what did he care? He was the spoiled darling of Monte Carlo and he had no time to be sorry for the women who gave too much and then discovered how frail, how inconstant a thing was the love of Nikko.

Janine knew the meaning of a jealousy so agonizing that she wondered how to bear it when she looked up at her partner tonight. The band was playing a slow waltz. Nikko's arm was about her. His fingers were holding hers. But so lightly that, although their graceful bodies seemed to move as one, he scarcely touched her.

'Nikko,' she whispered. 'I haven't seen you all day.'

'I know, dear,' he whispered back. 'I've been so frightfully busy — had dancing lessons all the afternoon. I wish I could spend more time with you, Janine. It's rough on us both. *So* sorry, sweetheart!'

He tightened his hold of her for a

fraction of a moment. Her blood leapt to his touch and his words. She told herself that she was a little beast to be jealous and huffy. Of course he had lessons to give. He worked very hard. Probably he got very tired and sick of it all — like she did.

'Can we have supper together tonight?' she asked him.

'Of course we will, sweetheart.'

'Do you still love me?'

His dark, handsome eyes opened wide as though with astonishment at the question.

'Of *course*, darling Janine. You know that!'

But he looked over her golden head with eyes that had grown bored. His one dread was being tied . . . tied to this girl, who was beautiful and fresh and charming . . . but who, as his wife, would make it difficult for him to have affairs with other women.

The waltz ended. Janine and Nikko bowed, hand in hand, and retired. The audience roared and cheered and brought them back. They gave an exhibition tango.

When Nikko's handsome, olive face bent over hers, Janine felt an overwhelming rush of love for him.

'Oh, my dearest — ' her lips framed the words.

'My sweet,' he whispered back.

Then she was happy. But half an hour later she was wandering on the moonlit terrace outside the hotel, the most unhappy girl in the world. Nikko had broken his word. He was not going to have supper with her after all. She had just this minute seen him disappear into a big limousine with a slim, dark-haired girl in a velvet, sable-trimmed coat. He was up to his old tricks. Another fancy. Jealousy cut like a knife into Janine's very heart.

It was a warm, fragrant night. But she wrapped her silver coat about her bare shoulders and shivered. Her eyes stung with hot tears. A dozen men in the hotel wanted to dance with her, dine with her, enjoy a tête-à-tête out here with her. She wanted none of them. She had given her heart to Nikko and she could not think of anybody else. She existed only for him. She knew she was a little fool and could not cure herself of the fever of her love for him.

She looked out at the Mediterranean. It was dark violet in the starlight — glittering through a maze of palm trees and flowers in the hotel gardens. To the left lay the Casino — ablaze with lights; and behind the hotel, the tall, dark shadow of the little Alps.

It was beautiful and glamorous, and this was the season in Monte Carlo. A few months ago Janine had been so proud of her job, so ecstatic about her love for her dancing partner. But now, there was only incessant heart-ache, jealousy and loneliness. Yes, she was horribly lonely — when Nikko was not with her. Who was the woman with the car?

Janine was alone in the world. She was at seventeen old for her age yet curiously untouched by the world. Men were attracted to her — found her adorably pretty and fascinating but she accepted the attentions of her admirers serenely and without losing her heart to any man — until she met Nikko. That was a year ago.

From that time onward, Janine's peace of mind vanished. Nikko — experienced and a little blasé — was enchanted with his partner and enormously flattered by her love for him. At the same time he was irritated by that curiously chaste streak in her. He realized that Janine would never give herself to any man save in marriage. He looked upon her as 'old-fashioned', and absurdly virtuous. He could not understand it. But because he was temporarily infatuated by her, he promised her marriage. And Janine believed in him and staked her whole heart and faith in what was, alas, shifting soil.

Out here, tonight, in the Etoile gardens, brooding over the affair, Janine asked herself if she was not foolish to be quite so faithful and so loyal to her lover. Perhaps it bored him. Perhaps he would wake up if she let him see that there were other men in the world. To make him jealous — ah — that was the thing — that would bring him back to her, whole-heartedly. She was sure of it. She began to walk back to the hotel. And she thought, childishly, passionately:

'I will make him jealous — I won't sit down and let him *walk* over me!'

That was what Janine's reason dictated. But her heart said:

'Oh, Nikko, darling, I don't want any man in the world but you . . . '

* * *

Janine had not far to go. In the vestibule of the hotel she half collided with a tall man in 'tails' and white tie, an opera hat in one hand. He bowed and apologized. Then he said:

'Do forgive me for saying so, but I watched your exhibition dance with

Nikko tonight. May I tell you how wonderful I think you are?'

Janine smiled back. She saw that the man who spoke to her was English, with that unmistakable air of breeding and dignity which suggests British public-school and the 'Varsity.

He was, perhaps, thirty; extremely good-looking in a totally different way to Nikko. He was almost as fair as Janine. His eyes were vividly blue in a face browned by the sun. He looked an athlete, clean, balanced, thoroughly nice. And he had the most charming smile which crinkled up those very blue eyes and softened a mouth which was rather stern in repose.

'It's very nice of you to tell me that you thought our dance wonderful,' said Janine.

'I didn't. I said *you* were wonderful,' he corrected, laughing. 'I don't dance, myself, or I'd beg you to dance with me.'

'I've no idea who you are — ' she began.

'But I know you. I've been watching you dance the whole evening. Surely the gods have sent you. You're unearthly and like a moon-goddess. Don't frown on me and vanish.'

Her lips trembled into laughter. Her heart-break, her disappointment in Nikko, flung her into a reckless mood. She played up to the attractive stranger.

'Tell me your name, audacious mortal.'

'Peter Willington, O goddess of the night.'

'And your habitation?'

He grinned at her, like a boy.

'Not the Etoile of Monte Carlo. I live in England. My home is in Sussex. I came out here this morning to stay with my brother and his wife. They've been at this hotel for a week. Derry, my brother, sent for me.'

'I see,' said Janine.

'Now, moon-goddess — your earthly name.'

'Janine O'Mara,' she said, smiling.

'Irish?'

'Half Irish.'

'That's why you've got eyes like Killarney's lakes — transluscent green,' he said promptly. 'What more can a man desire than to meet a moon-goddess with Irish eyes?'

She laughed again. She had to. Peter Willington was so gay, so humorous. He made her play up to him. She stood there, smiling and talking to him in the warm sunlight.

'Let's go along to the Casino,' he suggested. 'My brother's playing. We'll go and see how much he's winning or losing — shall we?'

'Perhaps — ' she hesitated, her thoughts still circling agonizedly round the thought of Nikko. Then she felt Peter Willington's firm fingers round her arm again.

'No refusals, moon-goddess. I'm determined to spend at least one hour in your enchanting and starry presence.'

Then she laughed again, a little

helplessly and found herself saying:

'Very well . . . I'll come . . . '

At that moment a car drew up to the hotel entrance. A man and woman stepped out of it. Janine's heart gave a peculiar twist. Nikko . . . Nikko had come back. The dark-haired girl was still with him.

'Hello!' said Peter. 'Here's Clare — Mrs. Willington, my brother's wife.'

So that was who she was! A married woman! Janine looked at Mrs. Willington and then at Nikko. She swallowed hard.

'Forgive me . . . I want just a word . . . with my partner . . . '

Clare Willington saw her brother-in-law frown and then moved toward him.

'Hullo, Peter,' she said carelessly.

'Where's Derry?' he asked.

The gaiety, the boyishness had left his face. His lips were a hard line, his eyes like blue stones. If there was one woman in the world he disliked it was Clare. She was beautiful enough, attractive enough. But Peter happened to know exactly how selfish and vain and greedy she was. He was devoted to his brother. Poor old Derry was a weak character — nobody knew that better than Peter — and he needed moral support. Clare would never give it.

'Derry's still playing roulette,' she said, shrugging her shoulders.

'Can't you get him away from it, Clare?'

'No. He won't listen to me. You'd better try yourself.'

Peter narrowed his eyes. He knew that Clare hadn't tried to get Derry away. She was much too busy amusing herself . . . with Nikko, the dancer, apparently. And Nikko meant something to Janine. That was plain to be seen. Peter had almost resented it when he had seen the light flash into Janine's eyes because Nikko had appeared on the scene.

Janine was talking to her partner by the car.

'Nikko — our supper — you promised — '

'I know, darling — I'm so sorry. But . . . ' he nodded discreetly toward Clare Willington. 'My client . . . valuable to me, you know, Janine. She's going to have a dozen lessons at top price. I want the money — for you . . . '

His hand stole out and gripped hers. But for once Janine was not comforted.

'Does it necessitate your having supper with Mrs. Willington?' she demanded.

'I don't want to offend her, dearest.'

Janine's heart beat fast and her cheeks were burning. She suddenly wrenched her fingers from her lover.

'If you go out with Mrs. Willington tonight I — I shall let Mr. Willington — her brother-in-law — take me out.'

Nikko's handsome eyes narrowed, but he tried not to show Janine that he was bored and irritated by her:

'Don't be silly, sweetheart — '

'Well!' she interrupted. 'Which is it to be?'

'I want you to enjoy yourself, my sweet. By all means go out with

Willington. It'll amuse you, perhaps. See you later.'

He was gone. Mrs. Willington with him. Janine stood still, trembling, a mist before her eyes. He had been just as charming as ever to her. He wanted her to 'enjoy herself'. So he didn't mind. He wasn't even jealous! Oh, she could die of misery. She loved him so. And he went off, smiling at that married woman.

Peter — watching her — saw and understood. With deep pity in his heart — he said:

'Come with me — let me take you to the Casino. I'd like to be a friend of yours, if you'd let me.'

She swallowed hard and tried to laugh, to be gay and proud.

'Thanks — I'd like it. You're very kind.'

He took her arm and walked with her into the moonlight and called for his car. Her bare slim arm felt cool and smooth as velvet under his fingers. A queer thrill shot through

Peter Willington.

In silence they drove to the Casino.

And in the limousine driven by Mrs. Willington's chauffeur from the hotel to the Casino Nikko and Clare Willington were in each other's arms. For a week they had met every afternoon; every evening; danced together; driven away, secretly, when Janine was busy with her own lessons; spent thrilling, glamorous hours together. They were lovers — madly in love.

Nikko had had many women infatuated with him but he had not cared to enter into any serious intrigue with them. With Clare Willington it was different. She was a woman of wealth as well as beauty. She could give him everything that money could buy. And Nikko was tired of his career as a dancer. He wanted ease and luxury — as well as a beautiful wife. Janine had nothing. She was as peniless as himself. But Clare had everything.

'If only I were free,' whispered Clare. 'If Derry didn't exist . . . '

Nikko's nostrils dilated. If Derrick Willington didn't exist. Yes — then Clare would marry him. The thought maddened him.

'Now, Peter, my brother-in-law has come and he'll hang round and watch and we shan't be able to meet so often,' said Clare. She put up a hand and smoothed Nikko's head. 'And your partner, Janine — she hates me — she's jealous of me.'

'Oh, I can manage Jan,' he said, frowning.

'Sure you don't love her any more?'

'*Mon Dieu*, yes. I'm sick to death of her. It's you — you, all the time, Clare!'

His hot lips touched her eyes with their heavy lashes; her ripe, responsive lips.

* * *

'*Rien ne va plus . . .* '

Peter Willington and Janine stood at one of the tables watching the game. Janine — tired and depressed — looked on with weary indifference. But Peter was concentrating upon his brother. He stood just behind Derrick; watched him lose one little pile of plaques after another.

'The young fool!' thought Peter.

But there was a very warm corner indeed in his heart for that young brother who was chucking away his money in such idiotic fashion.

Peter knew perfectly well that the boy was a bundle of nerves and had been since his unfortunate marriage to Clare who was older than himself and had never, from the beginning, been a suitable wife for him.

'If I could only help him,' thought Peter. 'He's drinking and gambling as an anodyne — and he'll end by ruining himself.'

He bent down to his brother.

'Chuck it, old man. Come and have some supper. Janine, the dancer, is with me — she's most charming. Come and meet her.'

Derrick barely looked up.

'Not just now. Let me alone, Peter. I've lost the devil of a lot and I must try and get it back.'

'Mugs' game, old man,' said Peter.

'*Zero*,' droned the croupier's voice.

Derrick lost again. He pushed another pile of chips recklessly on to the table. Peter shook his head.

'*Les six derniers*.'

Janine touched Peter's arm. 'Is your brother winning?'

'Losing heavily,' he said. 'I can't stop him. Janine, I hate this damn game.'

'So do I. I never play. Nikko does sometimes.'

Peter suddenly found himself resenting the name of Nikko, the dancer, on Janine's lips and neither did he relish the idea that the man was this girl's lover. He took her arm.

'Let's go and walk by the sea,' he said. 'The atmosphere in here's enough to kill you.'

'Yes, I'd like to go,' she said wearily.

With a regretful, backward look at his young brother, Peter walked out of the room with Janine.

He glanced at her when they were outside the Casino and descending the moonlit steps of the terrace. She was like a tired, white flower dropping on its stem, he thought. Very young she looked with the starlight in her shadowed eyes and on her fair head, turning it to silver. His heart was filled with curious tenderness for her.

'Why do you look so sad, Janine?' he asked her.

She shook her head. 'I'm not.'

'But you are,' he said gently. 'I wish I could help.'

'Nobody can help me,' she said in a bitter voice.

It hurt him to see a girl so young, so lovely, with that tragic look in her eyes. She should be laughing — not on the verge of tears — this beautiful child.

'My dear,' he said, 'we've only just met and we don't know each other very well, but I wish I could know you better. And in any case, there's no reason why you shouldn't let me be your pal. I'm a man. I understand things. If it's some fellow who — '

'Don't ask me — please,' broke in Janine. Her under lip quivered.

Peter's blue eyes suddenly narrowed. He stood still and took her by both small hands.

'Look here, little moon goddess,' he said in his gay, charming way. 'You can't deceive me. I'm not a blind fool. I can see what's happening . . . '

'But don't ask me about it — don't!' she broke in, flushing from chin to brow. 'I dare say it's I who am a blind fool — worrying myself about nothing.'

'Can't I help?'

'How can you?'

His fingers tightened about her wrists.

'Janine, I've known a good many women in my life but they've meant very little. For some strange reason — you do mean something. I'd give quite a lot to make you happy again.'

'You're awfully kind . . . ' the golden head dropped.

His whole body seemed to leap; to tingle. It was all he could do to restrain himself from catching her to his heart.

'What man could help being nice to you?' he said. 'Janine . . . '

'No — don't,' she broke in. She put out a hand and held him back because he would have moved toward her.

He flushed. His very blue eyes were almost black in the healthy brownness of his face. He was in love and he ached to take this slim girl in her billowing white frock, right into his arms and touch that adorable red mouth in a kiss. But he controlled the desire.

'All right, my dear,' he said. 'I won't. But I want you to know that I — I'd give the world to have the right to make you happy. I'm your friend, little Janine. But if ever I can be more — if you need me — tell me, dear.'

Janine walked back into the Casino with Peter. She thought what a dear he was! But Nikko had spoiled her for every other man.

She went into the cloakroom;

combed her shining head; powdered her face and then walked back to the elaborate doorway of the Casino. She had left Peter waiting for her. She saw a tall fair man with an opera hat at rakish angle on his head, go down the steps. That was Peter. She followed. He was nice and she liked him. The friendship of such a man would be staunch and comforting. She reached the lowest step of the Casino and felt surprised that Peter had not waited for her.

'Peter!' she began.

Then she paused. Out of the shadows another man suddenly appeared; a dark figure that moved swiftly toward the other. Then — the thing happened so quickly she scarcely had time to draw breath — something flashed in the moonlight. There was a report. The fair-haired man whom she thought was Peter Willington, flung up his arms and dropped like a plummet within a few yards of Janine. He did not so much as utter a groan. The man with the revolver vanished into the shadows as swiftly, as silently, as he had come.

Janine stood still, frozen with horror. She realized that a murder had been done before her very eyes. Then she pulled herself together with a gigantic effort and rushed forward and knelt beside the fallen man.

'Peter!' she choked.

She stopped. The opera hat had toppled from the fair head. She saw that it was not Peter. It was his brother, Derry. So like, yet so unlike. And now he lay there very still and marble-pale; arms and legs sprayed out grotesquely as he had fallen; profile outlined against the dark ground. His eyes which had glittered so feverishly in the Casino, a few moments ago, stared glassily and blindly now to the starlit sky. Janine put a hand to her throat.

'Oh, my *God!*' she sobbed under her breath. 'He's *dead . . .*'

She staggered on to her feet and began to run blindly towards the Casino!

'Help — oh come quickly — help!'

The elaborate doors opened. A crowd of people poured out. People came from all parts of the garden. Some had heard the shot. A murmur passed from mouth to mouth:

'*Suicide!*'

It was not unusual for a tragedy of this kind to occur in Monte Carlo outside the Casino. Many a desperate man, having staked his last *louis* and lost, has staggered down those beautiful white steps and shot himself beside the sea or in those lovely, luxuriant gardens.

Janine stood still, panting, sobbing under her breath, her cheeks as white as her gown. She saw Peter Willington pushing his way through the crowd which, filled with morbid curiosity, gathered and hid the tragic, prostrate figure on the ground, from view. Peter, livid under his tan, looked shocked and horrified. He passed Janine blindly. He knelt down beside his brother and picked up a little automatic which had fallen to the ground beside him. He fingered it in a dazed way and stared down at the piteous boyish face. He did not in this moment doubt that Derry had taken his life. He knew his weak impulses so well. He knew that Derry had been unhappy in his marriage; disappointed in his hard, beautiful wife, and that tonight he had lost a great deal of money.

Janine fought her way through the little staring, chattering circle of people and reached Peter Willington's side. He stood up and looked at her dully.

'You see — what's happened — my brother — ' he said in a husky voice.

'I'm so sorry — terribly sorry!' she stammered.

'Suicide,' said Peter in the same dull tone. 'Poor old Derry!'

Janine shook her head. Agitatedly she looked at him and then down at the dead man. 'No, — it wasn't — ' she began.

She felt a hand close round her wrist like a vice. A hoarse voice whispered in her hear: 'No, no — say nothing. For

God's *sake* keep quiet, Janine!'

She turned and was amazed to see Nikko standing behind her. His handsome face, always very pale, was a livid mask in the moonlight. There were beads of wet glistening on his forehead; on his blue-black hair. She stared.

'Nikko — '

'Come with me. I want to talk to you,' he said. 'Come, darling — for the love of God!'

Janine allowed him to draw her away from Peter Willington and the crowd. Peter's blue eyes followed the slim young figure in white, but only for an instant. His passion for Janine was a secondary consideration to this terrible thing which had happened to his brother. A *gendarme* with his little military-looking cape was approaching, followed by another. Janine heard the well-bred English voice saying, in a grief-stricken way:

'My brother . . . yes . . . shot himself . . . yes . . . yes . . . '

Janine turned piteously to her lover.

'Nikko — what is it? Why mustn't I say anything?'

'Let's get away from here and talk,' he said. He put an arm about her waist and drew her toward a deserted portion of the Casino gardens. They found a bench and sat down. Then he clutched at her and held her closely and leaned his head on her breast.

'Janine, darling, my sweet, tell me you love me!' he panted.

'But you know I do,' she said, astonished.

'Thank heavens!' he said, more to himself than to her.

As Nikko sat there, panting with relief because he had got Janine away from Peter Willington and silenced her in time, his feverish brain reviewed all that had happened in the last quarter of an hour. He was aghast — at himself. Aghast and horror-stricken because he had given way to the most terrible temptation of his life.

He saw himself leaving Clare Willington's side and, having seen her to her car, he had returned to the Casino and watched Derry Willington come down the steps. He had been raging, all the evening, against fate — against the fact that this weak, dissipated young gambler stood between him and the woman of his desire.

She would not run away with him. Would not stand the degradation of divorce, of having mud slung at her in the courts. She was too well known. The rich Clare Willington. In her way, she was proud. No — she would not elope with him. But all through that feverish evening, in between the passionate kisses, the broken love-laughter, the wild embraces, she had reiterated those words: 'If only I were free!' until Nikko's brain had felt like bursting and the sentence had danced before him in letters of fire. Finally he had left her, in a state of extreme agitation and passion — exasperated and jealous of the boy who had a right to join her in the hotel — to call her wife. And so — in a temporary fit of insanity — he had shot

Derrick Willington as he walked down the Casino steps. In an instant of hideous jealousy and rage such as might have shaken the soul of Othello — he had shot — to *kill*.

Then, to his horror, as he drew back in the shadows, he saw Janine. Despair had seized him. She must have seen. She must know. What could he do, now? He had bungled things badly. He had murdered Derrick Willington and freed Clare; but what good was that to him now? No use to be found guilty of murder and hang . . . Besides, Nikko loved life too much for that. With or without Clare, he must preserve his life, at any price. He saw only one way out. He must marry Janine.

He was relieved because Janine still cared for him. He took it for granted that she had seen him kill Derrick Willington and that her love for him conquered her aversion.

'You see, darling,' he said hoarsely. 'You must not tell the truth about this thing — think of the scandal — the disgrace — '

She stared up at his agitated face. To her, it was still the most handsome face in the world. She scarcely understood. She said:

'It wasn't suicide — '

'I know,' he broke in, shuddering. 'But say nothing. You must keep quiet. I ask you to.'

She did not know what terror prompted that appeal. She merely thought he wished to avoid the scandal which would naturally be attached to the affair if she came forward and stated that she had seen young Willington murdered. She was a dancer in the public eye; Nikko's partner. It would be horrible if her name became mixed up in it.

'I understand,' she said. 'I'll say nothing. But poor Peter Willington — he thinks it was suicide.'

'It's better — much better that way,' said Nikko feverishly.

Janine bowed her head. 'Yes — I see

— I understand,' she repeated.

He seized her hand and kissed it, then took her in his arms.

'Listen, my sweet,' he said. 'I want you to marry me at once — tomorrow. I'll get a special licence — and on Wednesday you must marry me. I've made up my mind — it isn't fair to keep you hanging round. Besides — I want you!'

Janine's whole face flushed vividly. Her heart raced. She looked up at him, her great Irish eyes gleaming with ecstasy. She had not expected this. All her heartache, her misery, her jealousy had been wasted and unnecessary. Nikko loved her. He had meant to marry her, all the way along.

She caressed his head with a small, tender hand.

'Oh, my dearest. Do you really want me?'

'Yes,' he said, and kissed her repeatedly on the lips and throat. But he was thinking: 'Once she's my wife, she'll never give me away. And a wife can't give evidence against her husband, anyhow.

'Listen, sweetness,' he said aloud. 'Let's get married quite quietly and secretly and say nothing to a soul.'

'Oh, Nikko — why?' A shadow fell across her radiant young face. 'I'm so proud — I want to tell the world.'

'I know, sweetheart — but it's best for our job — not to be husband and wife. We're dancing-partners — and before the world it's best to be just Janine and Nikko. Later, when our contract ends, we'll publish the news. Don't you love me enough to agree to that?'

With his arms around her she would have agreed to anything. She said:

'Yes, yes, of course. I'll keep it secret. Oh, Nikko — my love — to be your *wife!*'

* * *

That next day — the day when Nikko was getting a special licence — was not, on the whole, a very happy one for Janine. Her rapturous anticipation of her marriage, on the morrow, was shadowed by the inquest on Derrick Willington and her slight share in it. She had to tell the Coroner that she had found Derrick just after he had fired the fatal shot. She knew that she was lying and it worried her. It worried her to see Peter Willington's grim, unhappy face and not tell the truth to him. But the one face that mattered — her lover's — urged her to keep silence. Those dark, magnetic eyes of his never left her, while she was giving evidence to the Coroner.

The verdict was 'Suicide whilst temporarily insane' . . . and then Nikko closed his eyes to hide the triumph in them. Janine walked with him out of the stuffy little court and came face to face with Peter. He raised his hat to her. She wanted to stop and say a word of sympathy, but Nikko's hand drew her speedily away.

2

It was an ironic fact that almost at the same hour that Peter Willington grimly followed his brother to the grave, with Clare, looking her best in widow's weeds, a handkerchief becomingly pressed to her eyes; Nikko and Janine, the dancing partners, were made man and wife.

Very quietly, with utmost secrecy, the wedding of Nikko and Janine was contracted, in a tiny church up in the mountains. Janine thought it adorable of her lover to have arranged the most romantic wedding — not in a registry office in the town — but in that wee, rustic chapel tucked away amongst the olive-trees and off the beaten track. An old French *padre* conducted the ceremony. The sole witnesses were two peasants from a mountain village. Janine did not understand a word that the old *padre* uttered in his *patios*. And Nikko did not understand either. But they were married. And when Janine came out of that dim chapel into a blaze of sunlight, with a narrow gold ring on her finger, her happiness seemed too great to bear.

Only very much later that same night when Janine sat alone in her bedroom at the little, quiet hotel where she lived, she was struck by the thought that Nikko had seemed queer all day. He had been charming to her — all fire and passion and tenderness. But he had drunk a lot. While they danced at the Etoile, she had wondered if he had not drunk a little too much. He had looked white, his dark eyes had burned and he had laughed and joked with her a little wildly. Why? What was troubling him?

Janine stood at the windows of her room which opened out to a fragrant garden. She could see right over the trees, down the hill to the sea. Her heart was beating madly. The slim, beautiful figure in palest of pink silk nightgowns under an ivory velvet wrapper with swansdown at the throat and wrists, trembled a little. In a few moments Nikko, her husband, would be coming to her. All these weeks she had lived here alone . . . and this was still her bedroom only. Nikko did not want Monte Carlo to know they were married. He had taken a room here just for tonight. He was going to slip along the corridor and join her. Delicious, thrilling thought — a husband stealing to his wife's bedroom.

Janine's cheeks were as pink as the roses in the starlit garden, when she saw the handle of the door turn and a moment later Nikko stood in the room with her. She walked straight into his arms and hid her eyes against his shoulder.

'Nikko, I love you. Tell me you love me.'

'I love you,' he muttered.

'I'd lay down my life for you,' she said in a broken voice and wound her bare, slim arms about his neck.

Suddenly, he took those smooth arms and looked intently into her eyes.

'You'll never tell a living soul the truth about young Willington's death? Swear it, by God,' he said hoarsely.

'Not if you don't wish me to,' she said, and then her brow clouded. 'But it seems all wrong, the more I think about it. Nikko, what a terrible thing it was. Who should want to murder that poor boy? Who could it possibly have been?'

Dead silence. Nikko's heart gave a great twist. He went from white to scarlet, then livid again. He stared dumbfoundedly at Janine. He licked his dry lips.

'What do you mean . . . who could it have been?'

'Well — who *did* murder Derry Willington?'

'*Mon Dieu*,' Nikko said under his breath. 'Then you don't know?'

'No. I couldn't see who it was in the darkness. Do you know, darling?' she asked innocently.

His arms fell away from her. His lips

worked and his body shook with sudden terrible laughter. For he suddenly realized that he had no need to act the part of lover to Janine. That he need not have married her at all. *She did not know that it was he, Nikko, who had sent Willington to his death*.

'*Mon Dieu!*' said Nikko again. 'What a fool — what a blind fool I've been!'

Something cold and terrifying crept over Janine. Her expression changed from beautiful, innocent ardour to deep distress. She put a hand to her throat. Her heart beat so fast it seemed to hurt her.

'Nikko — what is it? Dearest — what have I said — what have I done?' she asked him.

He looked livid and terrible. He drew a hand across his forehead. It was wet.

'You didn't see the man who fired that shot at Willington? You're certain of that, eh?'

'Absolutely,' she said. 'It was much too dark. But I don't understand — '

'You don't know who killed Willington?'

'No — I keep telling you, no,' she said, completely baffled and deeply hurt by his sudden change of manner toward her. Her cheeks grew hot and pink and her eyes stung with tears. 'Nikko — my darling — I — '

'Don't 'my darling' me!' the man broke in, his fury getting the better of him. 'For heaven's sake, let's have an end to all this love-stuff. I don't want it. I don't want your 'Nikko darling' or your kisses. Do you hear? I'm tired of you. I've been sick of you for weeks. You might as well know it now.'

Janine looked as though he had hit her across the face with a whip. Her colour faded and she went dead white. For a moment, scarcely understanding the brutal words he flung at her, she stared up at the man she had married only this morning in such love and trust. She felt physically sick. Somehow she managed to speak but her own voice sounded queer and distant:

'Nikko — my *God* — what are you saying?'

He flung out his arms with a gesture of furious resentment.

'Do you imagine I married you because I cared for you?'

'Yes,' she said. Her eyes were dark with horror. 'Yes . . . '

'Well, I didn't. I married you to keep you quiet.'

'Oh, in heaven's name — ' she gasped, putting both hands to her heart. It hurt as though he were digging a knife into it — twisting it.

'Yes, to keep you quiet,' he repeated through clenched teeth. 'If I'd realized you didn't know who the man was I'd never have married you.'

'But what difference could it make to *you?*' she panted. 'What does it matter to you who killed Derrick Willington?'

For a moment Nikko didn't answer. He moistened his lips with the tip of his tongue. Then he laughed.

'No particular difference. But I thought you'd get mixed up in the case

— I knew it would ruin our reputations as dancing partners. I've got a living to make. I happen to be making it in partnership with you. Damn it, I've got to look after both our reputations, otherwise I don't care what the hell you do.'

'Oh, don't, *don't*!' Janine wailed. She felt she couldn't bear any more.

Nikko looked at the slim, tragic figure and the bent fair head without one shred of pity in his heart. He wanted Clare . . . and he felt he had been tricked into marrying Janine. The fault was his, but he did not care whose fault it was. He only knew that he need not have married Janine and he hated her. He lied — lied eloquently — to suit his book.

'I don't know any more than you do who shot Willington — but I understood you did know. Out of — er — consideration for your feelings — I didn't ask. But I wanted you to keep out of the scandal. I see now there wouldn't have been any scandal. You couldn't have told the police a thing. I needn't have troubled to shut your mouth by marrying you.'

Janine raised her head. She was so numbed with grief, with shock, now, she could scarcely feel any more knife thrusts. Her eyes — full of suffering — looked up at the man.

'So you really did only marry me — to keep me quiet?'

'Yes,' he muttered, averting his gaze.

She stared at him feverishly, as though trying to search for an explanation of this cruelty. And a horrible suspicion shot through her. She suddenly cried out:

'Oh, Nikko — it wasn't — it isn't — *you* — '

'What the devil are you insinuating?' he broke in loudly. 'How dare you — '

'No, no — of course not — it couldn't have been you,' she said, and hid her face in her hands again.

Nikko breathed more easily. For an instant his coward's heart had shaken with fright. He thought she had guessed the truth. And since she didn't know, he didn't intend her to find out.

When Janine spoke again it was in a hollow voice, and she did not look at him.

'Please — go,' she said.

'Yes, I'd better,' he said sulkily.

'I'm sorry,' she continued in the same flat, lifeless voice. 'Sorry you — married me — under a wrong impression. God knows I wouldn't have forced you into it. I — loved you.'

The man had the grace to flush. He toyed with the tassel of his dressing-gown.

'I'm sorry too, if it comes to that,' he muttered. 'But a man can't love to order.'

He opened the door. He was gone. Janine stared round her room. Mechanically she walked back to the bed. Mechanically she picked up a fold of the delicate pink negligée she had put on for *him* — bought for him. Her wedding-night — and the man she loved regretted his marriage and did not want her. Janine threw herself face downwards on the bed. Her arms were outstretched, like one crucified with grief. The pain, the shame, seemed intolerable — yet had to be borne. She only knew that whatever he was and whatever he had done, she could not stop loving this man.

* * *

Nikko spent a very wonderful hour with Clare next morning. In a delicate black chiffon dress which accentuated the creamy pallor of her face, and her dark hair sleekly waved, just showing two valuable pearls in her small ears, Clare Willington, the widow, looked her best. But the widow had no grief, no remorse in her heart for the young husband who had gone. She was crazily in love with Nikko. In his arms she took a dozen fresh vows to him.

'I love you — love you — love you!' she panted, strained against him; her arms about his neck; her heart throbbing against his. 'Nikko, you must never leave me now — you must come back to England with me — and we'll be married by special licence in London.'

'But, my beautiful, I'm only a paid dancer,' he said, with a hypocritical sigh. 'I can't take you — marry you — '

She stopped the words with a slim hand against his lips and said:

'If you love me — take me — '

When he left her, he was absolutely sure of her. He saw himself a wealthy man, with a beautiful wife and the world at his feet. Without a vestige of pity for the young partner whose heart he had broken, he made up his mind there and then at any cost to break away from Janine.

When Nikko determined to do a thing, nothing stopped him. He left the Etoile and took a hired car to the tiny chapel in the mountains where he had made Janine his wife. He found out where the old priest lived and then called at his cottage. He found, instead of the old *padre*, a young *curé*. Upon making inquiries, the *curé* told him that the old man had been shut away in an asylum yesterday.

'In an asylum!' exclaimed Nikko. 'But why?'

'He was insane, *M'sieu*,' was the reply. 'For many months he has had no right to perform any ceremonies. He was discharged from his holy offices but whenever he broke away from his keepers, he would go to the chapel and attempt to perform various ceremonies. Very tragic, very sad, *M'sieu*.'

Nikko's pale face flushed. His eyes glittered with excitement. He gripped the *curé*'s arm.

'Tell me — would a marriage service performed by this insane *padre* be legal?'

'No, *M'sieu*,' said the *curé*. 'But why — '

'Good heavens!' exclaimed Nikko interrupting. 'But he performed a marriage ceremony here, yesterday — for me.'

'I deeply deplore it, *M'sieu*,' said the

curé. 'I knew nothing of it. I was away in Cannes for the day. But I can marry you today — at once — and it will be legalized.'

'Thank you,' said Nikko. 'I will let you know.'

'No marriage performed by a priest who has been unfrocked, is a real marriage,' added the *curé*.

Nikko left that mountain chapel with the most savage exultation throbbing in his heart. What luck! What stupendous luck! His marriage to Janine was null and void. He was free. He could marry Clare after all. The very last thing he wanted to do was to marry Janine all over again.

It was Janine for whom he searched when he returned to the Etoile. He found her giving a dancing lesson to a French count who had 'booked' half a dozen lessons the night before. He waited until the lesson was over and then approached her.

'I must speak to you, Janine,' he said.

She looked pale and languid. It was

a hot summer's morning and the lesson with a tiresome man who could not keep time, had fatigued her. But her whole face lit up and her lips quivered in response to Nikko's words. He looked excited, pleased; more like the Nikko she knew and loved. Surely he was going to tell her he was sorry — and start all over again.

'Come and walk in the gardens,' he added.

'I'll come at once, darling.' she said.

She put on her large white hat and followed him into the sunshine. She was filled with indescribable love and longing for him. He was hers — her husband. He could not mean the brutal things he had said last night.

'Nikko — ' she began.

'Come and sit down and talk to me,' he broke in abruptly.

They had reached a lonely and beautiful part of the gardens of the Etoile. Here giant palms offered shade, and a marble seat had been placed at a cunning angle so that one could see a blaze of flowers and beyond, over the white terrace, the shimmering sea. Janine sat down and took off her hat. With a nervous little gesture she smoothed back her fair hair.

'Nikko — we can't go on like this — I can't bear it, darling.'

He sat down at her side and drew a cigarette from his case.

'You're right — we can't go on like this and we won't,' he said. 'Jan — last night when I told you that I do not love you any more — I meant it.'

Every shred of hope Janine had cherished of winning back his love seemed to die. She sat mute — staring before her.

'You meant it,' she repeated in a hollow voice.

'Yes.'

'But I'm still — your wife, Nikko.'

'No,' he said. 'That's just what I'm going to tell you, Janine. You are *not* my wife.'

She swung round to him, crimson, staring.

'What on earth do you mean — Surely —!'

'There was a mistake — a very peculiar one,' he said. 'We were married by an old *padre* who was insane — who had no right to perform any religious ceremony. I didn't know it at the time, but it is so. You can inquire for yourself. Our so-called marriage is null and void.'

Janine went on staring at him. She looked as though she had received a blow straight across the face.

'Oh, no!' at length she said in a stricken voice. 'That's absurd, Nikko. You're joking. It *can't* be true!'

Nikko lit his cigarette with precision and then flicked the match away. He shrugged his shoulders.

'My dear, it's hardly a time for joking.'

'I know — ' she gulped and swallowed hard. 'But, Nikko — my God, it *must* be a joke. You can't mean it. That we're not married . . . that our marriage wasn't *legal?*'

‘That is so, Jan.’

‘Oh, what does it all mean?’ she cried piteously. ‘Nikko, I don’t understand?’

‘I’ve told you’, he said. ‘The *padre* who married us isn’t any longer a priest — he was half-witted and unauthorized to conduct a marriage ceremony. The registrar told me this morning that our marriage wasn’t legal and that if we wished to make it so we must be married over again either by him or a proper, authorized priest.’

Janine stared at him. She could see now that he told the truth. It left her speechless, filled with despair.

‘You can find out the facts for yourself,’ he added.

‘And you — don’t wish to make the marriage legal?’

He averted his gaze and frowned — kicked a pebble with the toe of his shoe.

‘I think we had it out last night, didn’t we? I’ll tell you, quite frankly — there’s someone else I want to marry.’

She clenched her hands tightly in her lap.

'Who?'

'That can't concern you.'

'No — I see.' She gave a bitter little laugh. It ended in a sob, but her eyes were dry of tears now. It had gone deeper than that. 'Very well. You don't love me any more. You only married me because for some strange reason you did not want me to say that Derrick Willington was murdered — and now you are going to take advantage of the fact that our wedding was illegal and marry another woman. That's how we stand — isn't it?'

He moved uneasily. He looked very pale in the shade of the dark cypresses behind them. The word 'murder' made him feel a little sick.

'Yes — that's how we stand,' he muttered.

Janine stood up. She stared blindly at the sunlit gardens of the Etoile. The light hurt her. Her eyes ached. Every particle of her body seemed to ache too, but her mind, her heart, were numb.

Nikko flung away his cigarette-end and stood up beside her. He gave her an uneasy, frowning look. She looked so frightfully white and distraught, he thought. Of course she was desperately in love with him. He knew it. He hoped she wouldn't do anything rash. That would be so unpleasant.

'Jan — try not to — er — to brood over this,' he said. 'I — I've been a swine. I know it. But I — you see — I fell in love with someone else . . . '

'I understand,' she broke in. 'Please don't apologize.'

'And our marriage was a mad thing — I was crazy to have done it — I — er — just made myself believe for the moment that I ought to do it — '

'Oh, *please*?' she cut in passionately, hot and raw with resentment. 'Please don't humiliate me any further.'

'All right, we'd better let the thing drop,' he said. 'I'm sorry.'

The scalding tears blinded her vision now and blotted out the vision of that handsome, magnetic face.

'Goodbye,' she said, in a broken voice.

'We won't say good-bye,' he said. 'We shall be dancing together tonight.'

'Shall we? Yes, I suppose so,' she said drearily.

He coughed and frowned, then smiled at her again.

'By the way — although things are over between us — keep your promise — I mean — keep out of the Willington business.'

She wondered vaguely why that bothered him so. But she was too tired and heart-sick to care. She nodded.

'It's over. I shan't say anything.'

He came up to her, took her hand and lifted it to his lips with one of his graceful, charming gestures.

'Thank you — for being so nice to me always.'

Then he was gone. Almost before she had time to realize that he had kissed her fingers. But she shuddered from head to foot.

'I can't bear it!' she said aloud. 'God, God, I can't bear it. What shall I do?'

She did not realize, in her anguish of mind, that she had spoken aloud. She was surprised and startled when a deep voice behind her said:

'What can't you bear? My dear — what is it? What has happened? Tell me. Let me help — please!'

She turned and found herself looking into the very blue eyes of Peter Willington . . . the man who had asked her to look upon him as a friend . . . the one and only being left in Monte Carlo on whom she could rely.

Half distraught by her grief, and the shock of Nikko's revelations, she clung blindly to the hand that Peter stretched out to her.

'Oh, I can't bear it!' she repeated.

And then she was in his arms, sobbing passionately; her wet, white face hidden against his breast.

Peter let her cry. He knew that she was in some very deep distress and that she was scarcely responsible for what she said or did. His heart beat fast and furious at the sweetness of the contact, the lovely softness and fragrance of her in his arms.

At last the passion of grief spent itself. Janine cried no more. And she became aware, with acute embarrassment, that she was in Peter's arms. She looked up at him and saw only infinite kindness and understanding in those blue eyes of his. She drew away from him, her face one vivid flame of colour.

'I'm sorry — forgive me — '

'Don't say you're sorry. Didn't I ask you to turn to me if you ever needed a friend?'

She sank down on the marble seat; in the very place that Nikko had just vacated. She hid her face in her hands.

'It's good of you — wonderfully good. But not a soul on earth can help me now.'

He sat down beside her and took one of the hands away from her face.

'Jan — dear — don't hide your eyes from me. Look at me — trust me

— talk to me. Janine — you mustn't say nobody can help you. I can. I will.'

'Oh, how?' she moaned. 'How? You don't understand — and I can't tell you.'

'Then let me tell *you*. You've just been with Nikko, your dancing partner. He is your lover — isn't he, Jan?'

'In the accepted sense of the word, no. Theoretically, yes. He was,' she said. 'We were — to have been married — once.'

'And he's broken with you?'

'He — he's found out that he cares for someone else.'

'What other woman can he prefer to you?'

'I don't know. Some girl he has met here in Monte Carlo. I don't know who — '

'But the fact remains — he's broken with you.'

'Yes.'

'And you care so much, Jan?'

'Yes,' she whispered, bowing the fair, graceful head which Peter had admired a hundred times. He looked at it now and adored the charming twist of golden hair at the nape of the slender white neck.

'Janine,' he said abruptly. 'Will you marry me?'

The golden head shot up. Two startled green eyes stared at him, glittering still with tears.

'Marry *you?*'

'Yes. I love you. I fell in love with you the first night I saw you dance,' he said simply.

'I know you don't love me, Janine, but it might come in time, and until it does, I swear I'll never ask you for a single kiss. I just want you to marry me — and to give you the protection of my name — and have the right to look after you. I'll take you right away from Monte Carlo and this life you've been leading as a dancer. I've got pots of money, dear . . . ' He smiled. 'We'll travel — see the world — you shall have everything.'

She sat dumb, staring at him. He offered everything — indeed, too much.

And after Nikko, he was the most attractive man she had ever met. There was something most lovable and charming about Peter Willington's personality; in the strength; the straightness of his character.

'How can I take all that — and give you nothing?' she whispered. 'It wouldn't be right.'

'I'm satisfied — if you'll do it, Janine,' he said.

'It wouldn't be fair,' she repeated.

He held her hands tightly.

'I want you to marry me, dear. Say yes. Let me love you. You needn't give me a single kiss — unless of your own free will. You can trust me.'

She hesitated. Then she thought of Nikko and all the humiliation that had been heaped upon her and pride flamed up. She would show him she didn't care — she *did* care — but she would let him think she didn't. She flung back her head.

'Very well — yes — I will, Peter,' she said.

His blue eyes drank in the beauty of her, but he exerted all his control to keep himself from snatching her to his heart and kissing that alluring mouth of hers. He contented himself with kissing her hands.

'My dear,' he said. 'I'm terribly glad. And I won't let you down. We'll be married by special licence in two days' time. I have only one condition to make. I want your promise that you'll put Nikko right out of your life and give me a sporting chance to win your love.'

Janine winced, but she nodded.

'Yes, I'll — promise that.'

So — for the second time within a week, Janine O'Mara was married. But this time there was no mistake. Janine saw no reason why Peter should be told of her humiliating experience with Nikko, so she avoided the local registrar and asked Peter to arrange the whole thing in Nice.

It was Peter's one wish to please her; to make her happy, and he obeyed her slightest wish. The licence was procured in Nice, and it was in Nice that they were married — by the registrar. Janine found herself Mrs. Peter Willington — truly and legally married this time, and with a platinum ring on her finger which she could show to the world.

If Peter had had his way he would have taken her back to England after their marriage, but she persuaded him to allow her to carry out her contract with the Etoile until the end of the week. Two more days. The management besought her to do so. It was so difficult to fill her place at a moment's notice. And Janine thought it would be shabby to let the hotel down, so Peter let her stay. But he hated every moment of the exhibition dance. It was *his wife* in Nikko's arms . . . his wife. Damn the fellow . . . damn the way he smiled down into Janine's eyes as they danced. Of course it was all part of the game; every smile was studied. But Peter watched and hated it.

Janine felt indescribably confused in

her mind. This was her wedding-night. She was Peter's wife . . . and still Nikko's dancing partner. And still — shameful thought — she thrilled in Nikko's arms and wished the dance might go on for ever. But she was outwardly cool and proud, and a little elated when she told Nikko that she was married.

Nikko was thunderstruck.

'Married — to Peter Willington?'

'Yes — why not?' she said.

'No reason at all,' he said. But he looked none too pleased. He thought the elder Willington a stiff-necked, prosy, arrogant fellow. And wondered if Jan would ever tell her husband the truth about the younger Willington's death. He was astonished, too, that Jan had consoled herself so soon. She acted her part well that night. She did not let him see that she was agonized and that she felt it was wrong and wicked to love him still so much . . . now that she was Peter's wife.

She had moved her things to the Etoile, at Peter's request. He had taken a lovely suite for her on the first floor. As soon as her exhibition dance with Nikko was over, she went upstairs. She was tired and unhappy and wanted to shut herself away from everybody. Peter said good-night to her in the private sitting-room. It was difficult for him — madly in love as he was — to look at the lovely young figure in the long, white chiffon dress — know that she was his wife and this his wedding-night — but that she and her beauty were not for him. He had given his word.

He raised her hand to his lips.

'Good-night — little moon-goddess,' he said, using the name he had first given her. 'You are certainly an enchantress. Sleep well.'

She flushed and smiled.

'Good-night, Peter, and a thousand thanks — for everything.'

He was a dear. She liked him immensely. But when he had gone, the thought of Nikko returned, haunting her, hurting her.

Feverish, restless, she walked out of

the suite and down the corridor. She passed an open door; glanced in and was astonished to see the man whose memory pursued and tormented her. Nikko — sleek and debonair as usual — in a dark red satin dressing-gown. He was smoking a cigarette, looking at an evening paper. Janine's heart seemed to stand still. What was he doing here? He stayed at the other hotel . . . she couldn't understand . . . then he looked up sharply and saw her.

'Janine!' he exclaimed.

Impulsively, she walked straight into the room and stood before him.

'Nikko — are you staying here?'

'Yes.'

'You've moved, then?'

'I have. So have you . . . ' He smiled at her queerly. 'Have a drink — a cigarette?'

'No, thanks. I oughtn't to be here. I only — wondered why you were at the Etoile.'

'Almost for a similar reason to yours, my dear. I'm engaged and hope to be married in London next month. My delightful future wife is at this hotel. In fact we're a jolly party.'

Janine looked at the handsome, mocking face and suddenly hated him.

'Oh!' she breathed. 'I know . . . I know. It's Mrs. Derrick Willington. It's that woman . . . you're marrying *her?*'

'What if I am?'

'And her husband — only just dead — '

'That's our affair . . . '

She looked at him blindly. The beastliness of the whole thing — particularly of his conduct — surged over her.

'I think you're contemptible,' she said in a low voice.

'That's amusing,' said Nikko. He suddenly came up to her and caught her in his arms. 'You look delicious when you're angry. If you hadn't loved me so much I might have loved you more, *cherie*. I like a woman to be a bit angry. Give me a last kiss to remember — will you,

Madame Peter Willington, who might have been Madame Nikko?'

'No,' she said indignantly. 'Nikko — let me go.'

But he pressed his lips hard against hers . . . and suddenly all Janine's love for this man died. Died utterly. Passion walks hand in hand with hatred. And she knew in this moment that she loathed him. She had borne enough — too much. He was no longer the Nikko she had loved.

She tore herself out of his arms and rushed from the room, slamming the door behind her. She ran straight into the figure of a man. She looked up and saw that it was Peter, her husband.

'Peter!' she gasped.

He looked down at her with eyes so hard, so furious, she scarcely recognized him. His face was white with anger:

'What were you doing in that fellow's bedroom?'

'I — I — only — for a second — I — ' she broke off, stammering, completely taken aback.

'You gave me your word that you would end your affair with that dancing dago and give me a fair chance,' said Peter in a voice that cut like a whip.

'I know — I — but — '

'But as soon as I said good-night — left you — you went to him.'

'Peter — how dare you speak to me like this?' she demanded, suddenly annoyed.

The brown, good-looking face grew very grim. And Peter's blue eyes were grimmer. Suddenly he laughed.

'You broke your word, my dear. I shall also break mine. This is our wedding night. You are my wife. That man may be your lover, but, by God, I'll end all that finally!'

'Peter — ' she began.

But he lifted her up in his arms. He was tall and powerfully built and he carried Janine's slim, graceful body as though she were a child. Carried her along the corridor swiftly to her bedroom, entered it with her and locked the door behind him.

He laid her on the big wide bed which was flooded with golden light from the little amber-shaded lamp just above it. Janine lay there, looking at him in speechless anger. Her eyes were very big and her face as pale as the white linen sheets. She lay there, a glittering golden girl with her fair, gleaming hair and the yellow light spilling upon her bare arms and throat and the delicate chiffon dress.

'Look here, Peter,' she said. 'You seem to have lost your temper — and your sense of proportion. You can't do what you like with me even if you have married me. I trusted you when you said you could treat me as — as a friend only. I believed you when you said you loved me unselfishly. Seems to me I've been a fool.'

The man — madly in love with her — was in the grip of fiercest jealousy. Seeing her in Nikko's arms had, for the moment, robbed him of a sense of proportion. It was only natural — the natural reaction of a man who adores a woman and has seen her in another man's embrace. He gave a hard laugh.

'My dear, we've both been fools. I trusted you too. But you lied to me. You haven't any intention of giving up that dancing partner of yours. You thought it would be convenient to marry me and have my name and protection and meet him round the corner. Is that it?'

Janine went blind with rage. She wrenched her arms from his fingers and struck him across the face.

'Oh, you beast — how *dare* you?'

The hard little fists against his face seemed to inflame him. He laughed harder. And suddenly he lost his head completely. He caught the slim, young figure in his arms and held her against him. Crushing the gossamer chiffons, he held her until she could feel the hard hammering of his heart against her breast, hurting her.

'My wife,' he said. 'To hell with your lover.'

'He isn't my lover — ' she gasped out the words.

'He is — and he was.'

'Let me go. Peter, you'll be sorry for this.'

'No sorrier than I am that I believed you when you promised to stand by me and leave that dago alone.'

His fingers bruised her delicate bare arms and the ruthlessness in those blue, blazing eyes appalled her. This was a stranger, this Peter; this violent, passionate, angry man. She could not associate him with the kind, charming, easy-going man whom she had married. She tried to fight him but he was all strength and muscle and she hadn't a chance. She cried out:

'Peter — don't — please — it isn't fair — '

'You haven't been fair to me. I love you. I want you and by heaven no other man is going to have you, my dear.'

'Peter — *please!*'

He set his lips to hers and silenced her. The passion of his kiss robbed her of breath. But it also woke some answering chord in her that she failed to understand but which throbbed in her from head to foot. A strange wild tremor shook her. Her eyes closed. She felt faint and helpless, terrified of her own passions — roused in answer to his. When at length she tore her lips from his, he bent his head and kissed her throat and her shoulder — kisses burning through the pale chiffons. Her heart beat to suffocation.

'My wife,' he said thickly. 'Nobody else's. Kiss me. Kiss me, I say.'

She shook her head dumbly. He caught the loose strand of her golden hair and kissed that — and kissed her face through the silken veil of it. She had not known there could be such wild, passionate love. In her desire for Nikko there had been a quality of this, but she had not let it go too far. She had repressed it. There was no repression here. Peter was claiming her as his wife. She *was* his wife. And this was their wedding-night. In jealousy, in bitterness — primitive man — he held her in this embrace and she knew that she ought to resent it and hate him. But now the hatred and jealousy and resentment seemed to be consumed by the fire of passion that spread hotly over them both. She opened her eyes, looked up at him and saw that his strong face was transfigured. He suddenly laughed — but this time it was the broken, happy laughter of love.

'Oh, my dear!' he said. 'Sweetheart — *sweetheart!*'

She stretched her arms above her head and her beautiful body relaxed. A little shudder went through her.

'Peter,' she whispered. 'Peter, my dear . . . '

And the passionate tears suddenly sprang to her eyes and glittered on her lashes. He looked at her, saw them, heard the soft note in her voice and the ruthlessness left him. How could he hurt her, this young, helpless thing. He was ashamed of himself. The madness passed. Suddenly he reached up a hand and switched off the light. He no longer saw her goldness, her beauty. And his own face was blotted out from her in sudden darkness. But she felt his lips brush against her eyes; drinking her tears.

'Sweetheart — forgive me,' he said. 'I couldn't hurt you. I was mad with jealousy. If you tell me you don't love him any more — that you'll be faithful to me — I'll keep my word to you. I love you so. Worship you. Only be faithful — because the other thing is more than I can stand.'

She tried to speak to him — tell him that she would forgive him anything. She wanted, terribly, to tell him how his kisses, his caresses thrilled and excited her. But no words came. A strange shyness and humility seized her. Once more in the darkness she felt his lips against hers. Then he drew away and stood up beside her bed.

'I must go — I must . . . or I shall break my word to you. I've been a swine. Forgive me, loveliness, and good night.'

She sat up. She tried to say:

'Come back — don't leave me — '

No words came. And then she found herself alone. A shaft of pale moonlight pierced through a chink in the curtains and penetrated the shadows in her room. Blindly she stared at the dancing silver light. Then she turned and hid her burning face in the pillow. She ran her fingers through her hair. She whispered a name:

'Peter!'

Was she so fickle that she could swing from one lover to another like this? She felt ashamed. Yet there was no real shame in the thought that she was going to love Peter. He had married her, had chivalrously offered his protection and friendship, and asked nothing in exchange. Those few moments, held to his heart, breast to breast, lip to lip, had been a revelation to Janine. The old, wild passion for Nikko was dead and buried. Only a few cold ashes remained. But out of the ashes a new and much more thrilling love was shining — glowing.

There was no sleep possible for Peter that night. And little for Janine. But when the maid brought in her early morning tea, she also brought a huge bunch of roses, glorious scarlet blooms with the dew on them, freshly cut. With them was a small, sealed note.

> 'Forgive me for last night. It was because I loved you. I'll never touch you again until you come to me of your own free will. I love you.
>
> 'PETER.'

Janine buried her face in the scarlet roses and her cheeks burned almost as red. She looked up at the maid.

'Where is *Monsieur?*' she asked in French.

The *femme-de-chambre* informed her that *Monsieur* had gone out early with his bathing wraps.

'He has gone to swim,' thought Janine. 'When he comes back I'll tell him there is nothing to forgive.'

She bathed, put on her prettiest dress

and waited for him downstairs in the lounge.

Peter came back from his swim, glowing, healthy, with the brown of sun and wind on his face and the blue of the Mediterranean in his eyes. Janine looked at him as he entered the hotel and felt the strangest glow through her. A glow of pride in him. This was her husband — this handsome, athletic man whose head was almost as fair as her own — wet, glistening with sea-water after his swim.

He stood beside her for an instant.

'You got my flowers?'

'Yes,' she said. And there was a softness and invitation in those Irish eyes of hers that surprised him. He had expected her to be hard and angry. 'Thank you,' she added softly.

'Have you forgiven me?'

The woman's age-old desire to flirt, to coquette with her lover, seized Janine.

'Come down to me when you're dressed and I'll tell you,' she said.

His gaze drifted to the curve of her

lips. He went suddenly pale.

'Jan!' he said.

She turned away from him, red as a rose, and he ran up the stairs two at a time with sudden wild hope springing in his heart.

Janine walked on to the terrace of the Etoile. She thought:

'When he comes down again — I shall tell him I will be his wife — truly — and that I love him.'

She stopped short, and her lovely colour faded. A graceful young man in white flannels barred her passage. It was Nikko.

She would have passed him, but Nikko caught her wrist.

'Jan — I must speak to you,' he said.

'We have nothing to say to each other,' she began.

'I must see you, I say,' he repeated. 'Come and walk with me in the garden.'

'No — '

'Yes, you must, Janine, I'm in the hell of a mess.'

She saw, now, that he was paler than usual and that his dark eyes were gleaming, and he had an air of distraction about him.

'What is it?' she asked. 'What's happened?'

'I'm in a terrible mess over money.'

She stared at him. 'Why should your financial difficulties concern me?'

'My dear Jan — what a change! At one time any difficulties of mine concerned you.'

She coloured, but she kept her fair head proudly high. 'I'm sorry, Nikko. But times have changed. I am Peter Willington's wife. I want nothing to do with you.'

For a moment he was silent. His eyes glared at her resentfully.

Nikko was in very sore straits. A nasty shock had awaited him when he saw Clare early this morning. And she had received the shock first, and by post. A letter from her solicitors in England had informed her that she had lost every penny of her money. Most of it was invested in Australia. There had been a frightful slump — a panic. Her stocks and shares had gone down to nothing. Her property when it was disposed of would barely pay her debts, because she was an extravagant woman, and Derrick had died up to his eyes in debt. In other words, Clare Willington was a ruined woman. Sick with rage and chagrin she had wept in Nikko's arms.

'You won't desert me — swear you won't desert me,' she had implored him.

Nikko had felt equally sick with rage. He had been so sure of a life of luxury and ease, once Clare was his wife. Half her attraction for him had been the fact that she was a wealthy woman. Clare, penniless, offered not half the enticement. He had not had the nerve to tell her so. He had kissed and comforted her and told her he would be true to her; that they would find a way out. But he had his own financial worries. Since his affair with Clare he had spent recklessly; bought dozens of new suits; silk underclothes; hats; new studs and links; things he had craved with all the extravagance of his nature. He had also given notice to the Etoile. They were engaging a new exhibition dancer. He had not only got himself into debt, but he had lost his job.

'Look here, Janine,' Nikko said in a whining tone. 'You used to care for me. You won't see me ruined — bankrupt — will you?'

'You are trying to tell me you're in debt and you want financial help?'

'Yes,' he said.

She looked at him and realized how she despised him.

'After the way you treated me — how dare you come and whine to me for money?' she asked indignantly. 'To begin with, I haven't any and — '

'No, but your husband has,' he broke in.

Janine flushed crimson.

'Do you suggest I should ask my husband for money for *you?*'

'Listen, Janine,' he said, his eyes narrowed, his breath quickening. 'I'm in a hole — a damned bad one. And you've got to get me out of it.'

'Go to Mrs. Willington.'

'Clare can't help me.'

'Why not?'

'That's my affair. Anyhow, she can't. But you can and must.'

'Are you crazy? You know I haven't a penny.'

'But Peter Willington has. And I'm liable to rot in a French jail — and you know what they are like — if I don't find a thousand pounds this week.'

'A thousand?'

'Yes. I'm in debt to the tune of a cool thousand. Janine — you must ask your husband to give it to you.'

'You really are mad, Nikko. As if Peter would pay your debts. He loathes you!'

Nikko gave a nasty laugh. 'He loathes me, does he? Well, he's in love with you. He'll give it to you for yourself.'

'No. Never. I'll never ask for it.'

'You don't care a damn for me any more?'

'No, I don't think I do.'

'You've fallen for him, perhaps?'

'Perhaps I have,' she said proudly.

Nikko laughed again. 'And does Mr. Peter know that you were married to me . . . even though the marriage wasn't legal?'

Janine changed colour. 'I didn't want him to know. There was no necessity to tell him as it was not legal and we were never really married,' she said uneasily.

'But supposing he was told that we spent our — er — wedding-night *together?*'

She looked at him in a frightened, startled way. 'But that isn't true!'

'No. But what man is going to believe I didn't spend that night with you — as I believed you to be my wife.'

Janine's heart began to pound; to hurt her.

'Nikko — you can't mean this. You know we were never — really married — in any way.'

'No. But Peter Willington, if he's in love with you, won't credit that fact. He knew how crazy you were about me.'

'Oh, you utter cad!' she broke out, passionately.

'I'm sorry, but I'm up against things.'

'In other words — you're trying to blackmail me.'

Nikko shrugged his shoulders. 'Call it what you like. Give me a thousand pounds in cash — which you can easily get out of Willington if he's in love with you. Say you want it for jewels or clothes or something. Or I shall go and tell him the jolly little story of our marriage and the . . . er — unfortunate mistake that followed it.'

'I shall tell him the truth — ' panted Janine.

'But you can't disprove that we spent our wedding-night in each other's arms — remember that,' was Nikko's parting shot at her.

She found herself running into the Etoile — white as a sheet — eyes full of a new terror. For she knew that was true. *She couldn't disprove that fact*. Peter could find out from the registrar at Monte Carlo that a licence had been taken out by Nikko and that she had been married by the crazy old priest in the mountain chapel. And why should he believe that she had spent that night apart from Nikko . . . when she had, herself, admitted her infatuation for her dancing partner. She loved Peter — now — wanted everything to be all right between them. She could not risk losing him. Could not bear that.

'I'll tell him everything,' she thought, hysterically.

A few minutes later she was in the private sitting-room of her suite. Peter emerged from his dressing-room; amazingly youthful and good-looking after his swim. He gave one look of passionate appreciation at the girl he had married. How lovely she was; fair as a lily in her ivory silk tennis dress and a little sleeveless silk coat with her initials in a scarlet monogram over the little pocket. Just a touch of scarlet to tone with the scarlet of her perfect mouth.

He came straight up to her.

'Jan — dearest — you have forgiven me — for last night? I'm so afraid I hurt you — offended you unpardonably.'

She was silent a moment. She looked up at him, flushing and then paling again. The passion and longing in his eyes made her head swim. She felt giddy; breathless. She was sure this morning that she loved him. She wanted once again to feel those hard, ruthless kisses of last night . . . more than that . . . to surrender entirely to his love. She had meant to tell him about her unfortunate wedding with Nikko. But she *dared not*. He might suspect her; might believe what Nikko had to say and he would never forgive her for marrying him without telling him the truth. Never again would she know the rapture of his love.

Desperate, she stood there silently gazing up at him with her lustrous eyes. Peter suddenly caught the slim figure to his heart.

'Oh, my darling,' he said huskily. 'My *darling*.'

She knew, then, that she could not tell him the truth. She must keep silent.

'Peter,' she said, with a little sob.

'Forgive me, sweetness.'

'I love you,' she said blindly, recklessly.

'You love *me?*' he asked, amazed.

'Yes.'

'Me? But I thought it was Nikko . . . '

She clung to him, her slim body trembling violently and her arms about his throat.

'That wasn't love. That was just infatuation. I love you — Peter — nobody else.'

Exultation surged through him. The red blood showed through the tan of his strong face.

'Jan, Jan — is it true?' he asked.

'Yes,' she said. 'Absolutely true.'

'When did you find out?'

'Last night. Last night . . . in your arms.'

'Oh, Jan,' he said. 'My wife . . . my *wife!*'

He set his lips to hers in a hard, fierce kiss that sent the world rocking round her. She had thought of that kiss . . . wanted it . . . and it made her for ever his. She tried to blot out the memory of Nikko. She put up a slim hand and touched Peter's brown, warm cheek. He thrilled even to that light, shy touch. He made a cup of the little hand and pressed his lips to the cool pink palm.

'Oh, my darling, my sweet!'

'Dearest — I am yours — absolutely yours,' she whispered.

He caressed her hair for a moment and looked over the golden head, through the window, across the flower-filled garden, the white terraces, to the glittering sea. It was all beautiful and exotic and romantic. But a sudden nostalgia seized him for England. He wanted to take this young wife of his home.

'Loveliness,' he said. 'Shall we catch the next train to Paris and then to London town?'

She raised her head quickly.

'Why, Peter?'

'I want to have my wife in England, and to get away from Monte Carlo. It has horrible, painful memories.'

She knew he was thinking of his young brother and that recent tragic death which he believed to be suicide. A qualm of conscience writhed in her. Oughtn't she to tell him what she knew about that 'suicide'. Yet why drag up old ghosts. Best to let them lie.

'You know so little about me and my home, really,' she heard her husband saying, his hand still caressing her hair. 'I've got rather a beautiful old home in Sussex, my sweet. An old manor house, hundreds of years old, with mullioned windows and beams black with age, and a garden that slopes down to a lake. There are two swans on that lake. It's so peaceful there in the summer — so lovely. I loathe Monte Carlo. I want you to forget you were ever dancing at the Etoile and to remember only that you are my wife — and mistress of Lullion

House — my home.'

She was flushed and starry-eyed now. 'Lullion House: Peter, how lovely it sounds!'

'Shall we pack up and go back there, dearest?'

With all her soul she wanted to say yes; wanted the peace of that old-fashioned English home; wanted the old oak-beamed house and the English flowers and the white swans on sun-dappled waters. The forgetfulness — the wiping out of the unhappy, difficult days that had been before Peter came into her life. *But she dared not say 'yes'*. Could not go just yet. Nikko held her back. Her promise to get money for him. Until he was satisfied she dared not leave the Etoile.

She managed, somehow, to laugh. 'All the same, Peter, your little wife is rather fond of festivities. She doesn't really want to leave Monte Carlo just yet.'

Peter tried not to show his disappointment. After all, he told himself, Janine was young. A young girl likes life. Why should she wish to be tucked away in a lonely country-house? He must remember that she had once had a career as a dancer — applauded, flattered, successful and used to the limelight.

He mustn't be selfish and ask too much of her.

He hugged the slim, graceful body close.

'Little wife of mine, you shall do exactly what you want. We'll stay on at the Etoile a bit longer, shall we?'

'Yes,' she said and hid her face from him.

'Come down to breakfast now,' he said gaily, and tucked an arm through hers and led her from the room.

* * *

While Janine breakfasted at a little table on the terrace under a striped awning, and drank in the music of Peter's deep voice, Clare Willington had a stormy scene with her lover.

When she was up and dressed, she sent for him; a peremptory message which annoyed Nikko. It was all very well being ordered about by Clare when she was a woman of wealth and position. Quite amiably in those days he had allowed himself to be told to do this and that and come here and go there. He didn't mind being a 'gigolo', a lap-dog, especially when the woman had beauty as well as cash. But now things had changed.

He went to Clare's private sitting-room, however, in response to the message delivered by a page. Clare was pacing nervously up and down. She was exquisitely dressed in palest pink organdie; dark head sleekly brushed by her maid; face cleverly made-up; lips brightly rouged with vermilion. But her sherry-coloured eyes were red-rimmed as though she had been weeping and she looked what she was — a woman of thirty, this morning.

Nikko regarded her with sullen eyes. She said, huskily:

'Nikko, I had to talk to you again. You stayed with me such a little while this morning.'

'I'm sorry,' he said. 'But one has to be — er — careful. Your brother-in-law is in this hotel and I — er — daren't be seen coming out of your suite.'

Clare put a wisp of pink georgette to her lips; an apology for a handkerchief. She looked, miserably, at the dancer.

'Nikko,' she said. 'Tell me it makes no difference to you that I've lost my money.'

He looked at her, frowning.

'My dear, we talked this over early this morning and — '

'And you hedged and parried, every time I asked you what you were going to do. You kissed me — caressed me — but you didn't ask me to marry you at once — didn't tell me you'd look after me.'

A slight red burned under the pallor of his face.

'My dearest Clare — be reasonable.

You've lost your money. You admit you're two thousand pounds in debt. Well, I'm nearly a thousand quid down, myself. What's the use of our slopping over each other. It would be more sensible to discuss ways and means of getting clear of debt.'

She put a hand up to a mouth that trembled.

'Slopping,' she repeated. 'You call it 'slopping' when once — '

'Oh, don't nag,' he broke in.

Her dilated eyes stared at him. She was tasting a little of the callous cruelty he had meted out to Janine; to other women. So attractive, so fascinating when he chose, this Nikko. So brutal, so merciless when his passion was dead. Was his passion dead for her — already?

Suddenly she gave a low cry and flung herself upon him.

'Nikko — for heaven's sake — don't speak to me like that, look at me like that. I can't *endure* it! Nikko, tell me you still love me. You can't have loved me only because of my money — you can't be so beastly — so mean!'

His patience snapped. He snarled at her:

'Oh, go to hell, Clare. Quit this. We're both of us in debt — your damned money is the cause of all the trouble. If it hadn't been for that we could have got married. But I've lost my job, thanks to you. You made me chuck it and what can I do now? If you expect me to marry you and get myself further into debt, you're dead wrong!'

Clare ceased to cry. Every word he said cut her like a knife. She tore herself away from him. Running her hands wildly through her hair, she fixed her glittering eyes on him and screamed:

'You beast — you beast — you *beast!*'

'Be quiet!' he said angrily.

'Beast, beast!' she repeated hysterically, shaking from head to foot. 'So it was my money you were after. You didn't care a damn for me. Now I know, You dirty cad!'

He gave her a scornful look.

'I'm going,' he said, and turned on

his heel. But she ran after him and clawed at his arm.

'Don't think you're going to get off scott-free, you low swine!' she said violently, her cheeks red with rage. 'I'll get even with you.'

'You bore me,' he said, and shook her off.

'I'll get Peter to deal with you!' she shouted after him, like a fish-wife in her temper — wild, blind with fury.

Then Nikko laughed.

'Sorry, my dear Clare, but I doubt if your brother-in-law will help you, either to pay your bills or avenge your honour. He's got a wife to look after, now.'

'A *wife!*' she gasped.

'Yes, didn't you know?' His contemptuous eyes rested a moment on her disfigured, passionate face. 'Your charming brother-in-law married my dancing partner yesterday.'

Clare gasped.

'Peter — married — that girl?'

'He did, and no doubt all his cash and attention are concentrated on her.

You won't get a look-in.'

He laughed. The laughter maddened Clare.

'Perhaps there's another woman in your life now that you've finished with me,' she panted, 'or are you chasing your former partner again? You seem to like best what you can't get.'

'I've had enough of one Mrs. Willington — I shan't try my charms on another,' he said brutally, and slammed the door after him.

Clare Willington stared at the door, wild-eyed, shaking. Then she crumpled up; staggered to the sofa and flung herself down; face pressed to the satin cushions. She knew what it was to suffer in that hour. In her fashion she had adored Nikko. And she knew now that he had loved her only for her money.

Would Nikko go back to Janine, or was there another woman in his life, now that he had finished with *her*?

'I'll watch,' Clare Willington thought savagely. 'I'll watch him — follow him

— haunt him and I'll get even with him somehow.'

* * *

The hours passed gloriously for Janine that day. Golden hours spent with a husband who adored her. She wondered how she had ever existed without Peter; she knew that life and love had meant nothing until she had learned to love and live for him. But every hour was shadowed by the thought of Nikko. Treacherous; hateful Nikko.

She could scarcely bear the thought of asking her husband for money. But it had to be done. She shrank from it; put it off; put it off; until evening came and still she had not asked. And then Nikko passed her in the lift going up to her suite. Peter was buying some cigarettes, out of ear-shot. Nikko touched Janine's arm.

'You're not forgetting, are you?' he asked, giving her a significant look.

'Nikko — please — ' she began.

'I won't discuss it again,' he broke in. 'I must have the money. I'm broke, I tell you. Get it for me, or Peter Willington shall be told . . . '

'Lies, lies,' she said under her breath with hot resentment.

'But he'll believe them,' said Nikko, and passed on, laughing.

Peter came toward the lift. The radiance had vanished from his brown, eager face. His blue eyes looked hard as stones. He came up to his young wife and gave her a searching look.

'What was that swine daring to say to you? He was laughing — damn him. Is there some — joke between you?'

Janine went white. She could not bear that tone, that expression, from Peter.

'Oh, darling — don't be jealous — please. Nikko only — only — '

'You don't care a damn about him now — there's nothing between you — is there? Answer me truthfully, for God's sake, Janine!' he said with a note of pain in his voice.

They had reached their rooms. As

they went through into the sitting-room, Janine answered huskily:

'Nothing — nothing — I love *you!*'

He did not switch on the light. In the darkness he caught her soundlessly against him and took her lips in a long, desperate kiss.

Agonized, she lay against his heart.

'God forgive me, but I must get the money somehow,' she thought. 'I can't lose Peter now. He means too much.'

He kissed and caressed her for a moment, then released her and switched on the lights.

'It won't do for me to lose my head before dinner, Sweetness,' he said with an unsteady laugh. 'Go and put on your prettiest dress and we'll have our wedding-dinner. We'll pretend that we were married this morning.'

Janine seized a chance here.

'I haven't many pretty dresses,' she grumbled — hating herself for it. 'Peter, I do need some new clothes badly. For you, darling.'

He gave a happy laugh.

'I'll buy Paris for you — or Monte Carlo. Thank God, I'm a rich man.'

She blushed scarlet and added:

'Will you be horrified — if I — I ask for some money?'

'Lord, no. Aren't you my wife? I couldn't allow you to go about without money. What a fool I've been — not thinking of that. My poor little girl — '

He opened his pocket book and pulled out some crisp banknotes.

'Of course, you must need petty cash for odd things — and my wife isn't going to be a poor woman. Sweet, here's some to go on with. Five twenty-pound notes. A hundred. How much do you need?

Sick with shame, she took the notes and could have wept with chagrin, having to do so; to deceive him.

'Thank you — darling, darling Peter!'

'Tomorrow I'll give you a marriage settlement,' he said in his generous, impulsive fashion. 'I'll pay a couple of thousand into a bank in your name as a start!'

His generosity overwhelmed her, but she was terribly relieved. Two thousand! That meant she could give Nikko half — settle him for good and all.

She waited until she knew that Peter was in the bath, and then hurried out of the suite and slipped downstairs. She knew Nikko's habits only too well. At this hour, just before dinner, he was generally to be found in the American Bar, drinking cocktails.

She sent a page to him.

'Ask Nikko to meet me in the garden — no — on the terrace,' she corrected herself.

The page vanished. She walked out on to the terrace. It was a warm, starlit night. A crescent moon hung in the sky and silvered the sea. A night for romance. And romance waited for her . . . *real* romance.

She would put Nikko out of her life now — for ever.

He came out to her; handsome, suave, smiling. He was in good spirits.

'Greetings, most charming partner-who-was.'

Cold as ice, hating him and herself, Janine looked at him.

'Nikko, there can be no jesting between us. Let's get this beastly business over. You want money. Very well. Tomorrow you shall have it. My — my husband is giving me two thousand pounds and I'll draw half of that out and send it to you.'

Nikko's dark eyes gleamed at her.

'Good for you, *cherie*. You're a sportsman. Got any cash for me tonight? I'm terribly hard up.'

She had brought £50 in banknotes with her. With a gesture of distaste she pressed it into his hand.

'Take these . . . '

He took them and stuffed them in his pocket. The crisp crackle was very satisfying.

'Wonderful girl,' he said. 'D'you know, Jan, sometimes I regret we ever parted, you and I. You're looking adorable tonight.'

'Don't dare!' she said in a stifled

voice. 'Oh, how I despise you, Nikko. Go away — please — and let me be in peace. Give me your word that after tomorrow — when I give you the money — I never see you again.'

'Very well,' he said, shrugging his shoulders. 'That's agreed.'

'Thank you. Good night and good-bye,' she said. 'You shall have the balance of the money — tomorrow.'

She hurried back into the hotel, hoping to get to her room and bathe and change before Peter realized she had gone out. Nikko, whistling gaily, and thinking that he was in luck, strolled back to the bar.

Neither he nor Janine — engrossed in their conversation — had noticed that a woman had been slinking in the shadows of the palm-trees on the terrace. A woman with a tortured, ravaged face and lips bitten until they bled. Clare Willington had heard every word that passed between them. And she had seen the girl press the banknotes into the dancer's hand.

She went to her own suite, sat down and wrote a note to her brother-in-law.

While Janine was dressing — putting on the long, white chiffon dress in which Peter loved her best — he called to her through the door:

'Sweet — when you're ready, meet me in the lounge. I'm just going to see Clare. She's written an urgent note asking me to see her on business.'

Janine's eyes dilated. What did Clare want with Peter?

'I know she's had bad luck financially', came Peter's voice. 'Most of her money's gone. I can't stand the woman — as you know. But she was Derry's wife. I'll have to see she doesn't come to any harm.'

'All right, darling,' said Janine, in a low voice.

'Sweetheart — ' he called softly through the keyhole.

'Yes — darling?'

'I only live — to hold you in my arms.'

'Oh, Peter!' she said with a broken little laugh.

He went along to his sister-in-law's suite — humming.

Clare received her brother-in-law in her private sitting-room with a great show of friendliness.

'Do come in and have a chat, Peter. It seems so awful — now poor darling Derry is dead — that you and I shouldn't be pals — doesn't it?'

'I'm sorry,' he said curtly. 'It's difficult for us to be — pals as you call it, Clare. You're Derry's widow — you sent for me. I've come. Now what is it you want, because if it's money I don't see why I should do anything for you.'

Clare shrugged her shoulders and moved away from him. She drew her short silver coat closely about her; nestling her cheek against the rich sable collar.

'Oh, don't bother to be nice, Peter,' she said airily. 'I don't want an unwilling friend. There are plenty *willing* to be nice to me.'

'Quite so,' said Peter coldly. 'May I smoke?'

'Do.'

She watched him through her lashes while he lit a cigarette. Against her will, she thought:

'He's damn good-looking and he's got a will like iron. He's worth one hundred per cent of Derry . . . but I'll make him suffer for being so rotten to me.'

'Now, Clare,' said Peter. 'Will you tell me why you sent for me?'

'Very well,' she said, balancing herself on the arm of a chair. 'Look here, Peter, you married Janine, the hotel dancer, some short while ago — didn't you?'

He stiffened. 'I did.'

'Know anything about her — her past, I mean?'

Peter's vivid eyes narrowed and his whole figure became tense with antagonism.

'Aren't you being — impertinent?'

'Am I?' She smiled charmingly. 'No — merely asking you. Did you know anything about this Janine when you married her?'

'That,' said Peter, 'cannot concern you.'

'But it does.'

'In what way?'

'You are my brother-in-law and I — er — I feel a certain duty toward you.'

'Duty toward me?' he echoed, then laughed. 'That's humorous, Clare.'

She flushed and clenched a hand.

'It may not strike you as being so humorous when I warn you that you married a girl with a very unsavoury past.'

Peter pitched his cigarette into the grate. He was white.

'If you were a man, Clare, by God — '

'No use flying off the handle with me,' she broke in. 'I'm only warning you.'

'I refuse to hear a word against my wife.'

'Oh,' said Clare. 'Then you know, perhaps, that she met Nikko, her ex-partner and lover in the gardens an hour ago and handed him £50 in notes.'

Peter's heart seemed to stop beating. Then it raced along; hurting him. His eyes were blue slits of rage. But there was also fear in his heart.

'It's a lie, you — '

'All right — if it's a lie — ask her — ask your charming wife if she gave Nikko the money and see what she says.'

'It isn't true,' said Peter furiously.

'I saw her — saw her give it to him. I wanted to warn you — put you on your guard — that's all. Repay my kindness by calling me a liar — I don't care!' Clare struck a match with fingers that shook and lit a cigarette for herself. She blew a cloud of smoke toward Peter, scornfully. 'I've told you what I saw, and I heard her promise to give him a thousand pounds tomorrow. Does that seem all in order? For your newly-made wife to be presenting an ex-lover with such a large sum of money?'

Peter stood still, breathing heavily, for a moment. And fear and indignation both blazed in him. Oh, God, he thought, could it be true? It was a dastardly thing to tell him . . . and yet . . . he had given Janine money at her own request and had promised her two thousand pounds tomorrow. On top of that she had met Nikko and paid him half what he had given her, tonight.

He looked Clare in the eyes. 'Why have you told me this?'

She averted her gaze. 'To warn you.'

'No — you've some other motive, my dear Clare.'

'If I have — it's my own affair.'

'Thank you,' he said bitterly.

He walked out of the room and shut the door behind him. Clare smoked furiously . . . staring after him . . . her sherry-coloured eyes full of passionate, tears.

'Now,' she said through her teeth, 'now, my dear Nikko . . . perhaps I've queered your pitch — and yours, too, my dear Janine . . . '

Peter marched into his sitting-room. He was shaking . . . shaking with nerves. What Clare had told him was sufficient to play havoc with the strongest nerves. He loved Janine and trusted her. To find out that she was double-crossing him . . . financing a man whom she admitted she had once loved . . . behind his back . . . It was intolerable. An insult to him, her husband.

Janine was just about to go down to the lounge. Not too happy; not too certain of why Clare Willington had sent for Peter.

She looked up at her husband with a timid smile. The very timidity of it made his heart sink. He fancied he read guilt in that smile . . . guilt in the green limpid eyes under their thick lashes. Oh, how lovely, how desirable she was, this young wife of his! And was it true that she lied to him — betrayed him.

'What's the matter, darling?' she asked. But she knew, from the way in which he stared that some disaster had befallen her.

'Come inside — I want to speak to

you, Janine,' he said.

She followed him back into the room. He shut the door and faced her, his arms folded across his chest, his handsome face stern and suspicious. The very suspicion on it cut her heart in two.

'Janine,' he said in a queer voice, 'I wonder if you would mind giving me back those notes I gave you just before we dressed for dinner. I — I find I want some cash.'

Her heart missed a beat. He, watching closely, saw sheer terror spring into her eyes and his last shred of belief in her innocence vanished. But he stood still, waiting for her to reply.

'I — why of course,' she stammered. 'H-how much?'

'All of it,' he said in that strange, cold voice. 'The whole hundred . . . '

She breathed quickly. Her face flushed and paled and flushed again.

'I — Peter — I'm so sorry — I — I've spent — £50.'

'On? On what, Janine?'

'I — on — I — ' she floundered wildly and stopped, swallowing. Her heart-throbs hurt her . . . pounding . . . pounding . . .

Then she heard her husband's voice, ice-cold; the voice of a stranger:

'Hadn't you better tell me the truth?'

'Very well,' she said tonelessly. 'I see — you know. I — gave Nikko the £50.'

'Why?'

'He — wanted money.'

'And why should *my* wife give him money?'

'Peter, Peter, don't speak to me like that!' she cried.

'I ask you why *my* wife should give Nikko money?' he repeated in a terrible voice. He was half mad with jealousy and disappointment. It was a bitter hour for him, for he had trusted her. 'When you married me, Janine, you swore to put that dago out of your life. You gave me your solemn vow to do so. And so short a time after our marriage you go behind my back, meet him secretly in the grounds of the hotel and give him money — money which you asked me for — for yourself.'

'Oh, heavens, who told him . . . how did Mrs. Willington know?' Janine asked herself helplessly.

'Answer my question, Janine,' said Peter stormily. 'Why should you give Nikko money?'

She put a hand to her head.

'He — needed some — I — '

'Don't trouble to lie any more,' broke in Peter. His temper was out of control now, and his whole body was shaking violently. 'There's only one reason for it. *You two are still lovers!*'

Janine stared at him, every nerve in her body jarred. Then she said in a broken voice:

'Peter, you're wronging me. Before heaven you are. I don't love Nikko. I don't love any man on earth but you.'

'I'm sorry. I don't believe you. But first of all, before I do anything else on earth, I'm going to wring the truth out of that hound, Nikko . . . '

He turned on his heel. Janine,

terrified by the expression in his blazing eyes, tried to stop him.

'Peter — don't — oh, *Peter!*'

He waved her aside, walked out of the room and shut the door behind him.

She stumbled to a chair and sank into it and hid her face in her hands. A wave of despair engulfed her. This then was the end of her dream, her hope, of love and happiness with Peter; the end of any glorious future which they might have had together.

Peter and Nikko came face to face in the crowded, brilliantly-lit lounge of the Etoile. It was impossible to make a scene in public, and Peter's anger and jealousy had to cool down. He waylaid the dancer who gave one glance at his white, set face and would have slunk by.

'One moment. I want a word with you.'

'Hell,' said Nikko under his breath. He was always — though he would not have admitted it — in secret terror that his crime would be discovered and that

Peter would one day know that he had murdered Derrick Willington and call upon him to pay the penalty. Guilt lived continually in Nikko's cowardly heart. But he tried to smile at Peter in a nonchalant way.

'Anything I can do . . . '

'Yes. You can answer to me for your secret meeting, an hour or two ago, in the grounds of this hotel, with my wife, and the fact that she gave you £50 in banknotes. I want an explanation of that.'

Peter spoke quietly — so quietly that anybody in the crowded lounge, where gay groups gathered for cocktails — might have imagined he was discussing the weather with the famous and good-looking dancer. But Nikko felt the knife-edge behind the softness of that voice. And he thought, in panic:

'Who, in God's name told Willington that? How did he find out? Janine couldn't have been such a little fool as to blub . . . '

Peter's next words dispelled that idea.

'I found out — apart from my wife — although she has now owned to it. Answer me, please. What explanation have you to offer?'

Nikko fingered his white tie. His cunning brain worked swiftly. Somebody — he knew not who — had sneaked. But Janine hadn't explained. Very well, he would put his own explanation upon it. He wouldn't tell Willington the truth, otherwise all his chances of blackmailing Janine in the future would vanish. He was badly in need of money. He must keep Janine in the hollow of his hand. His lips curved into a sad smile.

'Ah, Willington,' he said. 'I'm sorry you found out about this . . . '

'I don't doubt it,' said Peter between his teeth and had a sudden longing to knock the fellow down, there and then in that lounge, and smash that handsome, sleek face to a pulp. He loathed the dancing dago . . . and half his loathing was born of primitive jealousy because he loved Janine and resented her former passion for Nikko.

'You don't quite understand,' said Nikko in a low voice. 'I don't know what construction you've placed on this money business, but I can tell you the truth. Poor *petite* Janine didn't want you to know. She was so ashamed . . . '

'Ashamed . . . of what?'

'The fact that she had once borrowed from me.'

'Borrowed from *you?*'

'Yes. In the old days — ages ago — when we were partners — Janine was hard up — pressed for cash and I loaned her £50. Her one ambition has been to pay it back. She paid it, this evening. She said to me: 'Nikko, this is the end of our friendship because I love my husband — but I want to get free of my debt.' Poor little girl . . . '

Nikko sighed and shook his head.

'I didn't want to take the money, Willington, but she insisted, and as it made her feel square with me, I did so.'

Peter stared. And suddenly, a whole

load of suspicion, of rage, of jealousy, fell away from him. His spirits soared up. He was ashamed of himself. Good lord! So *that* was the explanation. And she had been too ashamed to own up to it. Poor Janine!

Peter's face was hot and his blue eyes kindled. He looked at the dancer without hatred now.

'I see — I understand. I've been a fool. That's all right. Stick to the fifty quid, of course. Thanks for telling me.'

'Not at all. Sorry if you were upset about it,' said Nikko. 'Now if you'll excuse me — a lady is waiting . . . ' He moved away.

Peter turned and went back to his suite — thoroughly ashamed of himself. The fellow wasn't so bad. And he, Peter, was a jealous idiot. Damn Clare for putting ideas into his head; for working so insidiously on his emotions. He burst into the sitting-room where he had left his wife. He found her sitting in a chair, staring before her with a heart-broken look in her beautiful eyes.

To her amazement, Peter's brown face was eager and happy again, and he fell on one knee at her feet, seized her hands and carried them to his lips.

'Sweetheart — oh, sweetheart — forgive me. What a fool — what a jealous swine I've been. I'm damned sorry, darling — honestly. Will you try and understand and forgive me?'

The colour rushed to her cheeks. She sat up, her heart thudding.

'What — why?' she stammered.

'Nikko explained, my dear — about the old debt. Why didn't you tell me, foolish child? Why didn't you say you'd borrowed from him at one time and wanted to get square? I'd have settled the debt for you at once. Were you afraid of me? My Sweet — am I such a brute as all that?'

He drew her, unresisting, into his arms. She lay against his heart, her eyes closed, and felt his kisses on her hair, her lips, her throat. She thought, confused, astonished:

'So that's what Nikko has told him!

He's saved me. But why? Is it only to work fresh mischief?'

She didn't know. She didn't much care. She was too relieved to find the danger averted; the crisis over. She was conscious only of happiness to find herself in Peter's arms again and know that he was once more her ardent lover.

3

It was a warm, June afternoon, two weeks later, when the aeroplane from France, containing Mr. and Mrs. Peter Willington amongst its passengers, landed at Croydon Aerodrome. Peter's own car and chauffeur met them. They had decided to spend a night in town, because Peter had some business on hand, then tomorrow they intended to drive down to Sussex; to Lullion House, Peter's beautiful Elizabethan home.

During those fourteen days — since they had left the South of France — rushed off 'like an eloping couple' as Peter had gaily remarked — Janine had known supreme happiness. She had felt, as they left the exotic South behind them and neared Paris, that they had also left the shadows behind and come into sunlight. The sunlight of happiness.

It was raining when they landed at Croydon. Who cared if it rained all day, or if England hadn't the glamour of Monte Carlo and Paris? It was England — Peter's home — *her* home.

They had spent longer than they had intended in Paris. A fortnight of enchantment. And that first night of their arrival, Peter had climbed with Janine, as he had promised her, to the starry heights. He had shown her all the glory of the world — and hers had been the magic of the sun and the moon and all the wonders of the earth.

Since that fortnight's honeymoon, his devotion for her had increased and Janine lived only for him. They were absurdly happy when they reached London and drove to Peter's service-flat in Berkeley Street.

'Just one night here, darling, and then Lullion House and we'll settle down and become a domesticated old couple,' he chaffed her in the car.

That afternoon he had to leave Janine alone. He had a business appointment with his solicitors, concerned with the executorship of his brother Derrick's estate. Janine, not wishing to go out, stayed in the flat and amused herself with Peter's books and gramophone. She was immensely thrilled because she was here, in his bachelor flat — as his wife.

It was like a black thunderbolt falling on the house of her happiness and destroying it utterly when a man-servant belonging to the service-flats, ushered a visitor into the drawing-room, just after tea.

'A gentleman to see Mrs. Willington . . . '

Janine stood rigid, staring. Nikko walked into the room. Nikko — handsome, sleek, suave as ever — yet somehow out of place in this staid, thoroughly British room of Peter's. His double-breasted waistcoat was just a shade too tight; his shoes too pointed; his suit — a pale striped blue — too dandified.

Janine stared and knew that she

loathed and despised him. Like a snake he curled himself into her garden of Eden. And she had thought herself safe from him . . . free.

'You!' she said. And there was a sick look in her eyes.

Nikko bowed from the waist.

'Dearest ex-partner. It's delicious to see you in London. And how are you and how's the marriage getting on?'

'How — how dared you come here . . . follow me here?' she stammered.

He raised an eyebrow in sardonic fashion. How very well and pretty Janine was looking in her flowered, greeny frock which brought out all the green in her eyes. She seemed to have fallen on her feet, marrying Willington. The place reeked of money. Expensive flowers, luxurious apartments; everything she wanted. Nikko was badly in debt. He had quarrelled finally with Clare. Clare was hard up, anyhow. Nikko wanted money. And he wasn't going to let Janine get everything.

'Nice little nest you've got here,' he

said, glancing round the handsome room.

'Please go — at once,' said Janine in a low, trembling voice. 'You have no right to be here.'

'You had no right to quit Monte and do me out of my thousand which you promised,' he said, his eyes narrowed. 'I soon discovered you'd gone, and followed, *ma chére*. I guessed you would eventually come to London. And I had only to look in the telephone directory to find Willington's address. It wasn't difficult to trace you.'

'And now you're here — what do you want?'

'You know.'

'It's still — blackmail, then!'

'Won't you call it helping an old pal whom you once cared for,' he said in a silky voice.

Janine's cheeks were hot and her eyes hard and bright.

'I won't be bullied by you, Nikko.'

'Come, come — I saved you from a jealous husband's wrath, in Monte,' he broke in. 'You owe me that.'

'Yes, but I won't give you my husband's money.'

'Then I'll tell Willington that you're *my* wife and not his . . . '

'That's a lie.'

'He'll believe it.'

'No,' said Janine in a strangled voice. Then she suddenly turned and darted through a door which communicated with another room — her bedroom. She had a crazy idea of locking herself into it; of showing Peter, if he came back, that she wanted to get away from Nikko.

But Nikko moved as swiftly as she did. She found herself in the bedroom with him. He gripped her wrists and laughed down into her eyes.

'You can't escape me, my dear. Now, look here, be sensible. Promise me that thousand — and I'll clear out.'

'Can't you leave me alone?' she moaned.

'You're so damned pretty — much more attractive than you used to be.

I've half a mind to ask for one of those sweet kisses you used to give me — as well as for the money — *cherie!*'

'*Oh!*' said Janine in a furious, panting voice.

He caught her in his arms and set his lips to her unwilling mouth — suddenly intoxicated with her beauty, her allure.

Peter Willington, coming quietly into his flat and into the sitting-room, saw through the open door, his wife in the arms of a man who, for an instant, he did not recognize. Then Nikko released Janine and swung round, and Peter saw who it was. He went livid under his tan.

Janine, pale as death, looked at her husband's livid and furious face. Her heart sank — like a stone.

'He's bound to misunderstand,' was her first anguished thought. 'Oh, *God*, why did this brutal thing happen?'

Nikko was none too pleased at the interruption. He had not expected to come face to face with Janine's husband. He had merely wished to scare Janine into giving him money, use common blackmail to secure the means to pay his debts and start again. Now his plans were doomed to failure. Peter Willington had come home too soon. And Nikko — coward that he was — quaked when he saw the seething fury in the other man's eyes. Peter looked dangerous. Nikko did not wish to risk his charming face being reduced to pulp.

Janine, with another agonized look at Peter, thought:

'He's mad with jealousy — he'll *kill* Nikko — and it will be my fault. I mustn't let that happen — '

Just as Peter sprang, uttering a savage, almost animal cry of rage, she sprang too, and leaped in front of him, her arms outstretched.

'No — wait — wait — listen — '

Peter — half off his head with fury — with bitter disappointment in her — literally snarled at her:

'Get out — get out of my way . . . '

'No — for heaven's sake — Peter — '

'Defend your lover, would you — you little — '

The word was lost because Janine smothered it with a cry.

'Peter — it isn't true — you're wronging me — oh, wait!'

He seized her shoulders and flung her on one side. But the delay had just given Nikko the time he needed. The dancer by this time was shivering, green about the gills. He gave one feverish look round Janine's bedroom and saw another door. He rushed through it and found himself in a white-tiled bathroom. Out of that led another door — into the passage. And then Nikko, hatless, leaving his stick behind him, tore through the front door and down the stairs to the main hall. He was safe. He hurled himself into a passing taxi and gave the name of his hotel. Leaning back, he wiped his wet face and neck and shuddered.

'That was a near shave — ye gods! The brute thinks I'm Jan's lover — he would have killed me. Damn it all! It's spoiled my game . . . *damn it!*'

He gnawed at his finger-nails, his handsome face a mask of rage. But — afraid of Peter Willington though he was — he registered a vow to get that thousand pounds somehow.

In Peter's service-flat there was a terrible silence for several minutes after Nikko's undignified retreat. Janine lay half-fainting across the bed; nursing her left arm which Peter had bruised when he flung her away from him. Her piteous eyes were riveted on her husband. He stood in the centre of the room, staring at the door through which Nikko had vanished. Passion seemed to have died in him. But something more awful than hot passion remained. A cold, sullen rage which showed in his white, stony face; in his tight lips.

Janine's eyelids closed. A little moan escaped her. Then Peter turned his cold, terrible gaze upon her.

'Get up,' he said.

She rose slowly to her feet. He looked

her up and down and there was a contempt about that glare crueller than death to the girl who loved him better than any living being on earth.

'And you are my wife,' he said slowly. 'You are the woman I married and swore to love and cherish until death parted us. *You* are the one person in this world on whom I would have staked my life — in whom I believed — whom I trusted — whom I would have defended with my last breath. *You* . . . '

She broke in with a low cry.

'Peter, you're wronging me . . . stop . . . '

'What was that man doing here?'

'He — wanted to see me.'

'Obviously. Followed you from Monte Carlo — couldn't keep away from you two short weeks!' Peter laughed — not a very pleasant laugh.

Janine put a hand to her aching head. She asked herself, desperately, what she could do. For it seemed to her that whatever she said, she must appear in the wrong. She would seem guilty. If she told the truth — said that Nikko was black-mailing her — that she had married him and that the marriage had been null and void — Peter would think the worst. He thought the worst now. She was between the devil and the deep sea.

She heard Peter's cold, accusing voice.

'Listen to me, Janine. If ever I find you with that man again I'll kill him. Yes, by God, I'll shoot him down like a dog. If he hadn't sneaked away like a filthy coward, just now, I think I'd have killed him today.'

Janine's eyes, full of hopeless misery, stared up at the hard, unyielding face.

'Peter, if only you understood,' she whispered.

'As for you,' he added, 'don't ever tell me again that you love me, Janine. I shall never believe you.'

She did not answer. Helplessly she sat there, twisting her slim hands in her lap. Tears gushed from her eyes. Every word he said wounded her to death. Yes, it was like death to her to know that he would not believe in her love.

'Do you want me to pack up and — go?' she asked in a low, miserable voice. 'Would you rather I — left you?'

He misunderstood and gave a bitter laugh.

'So that you can go back to that dancing swine?'

'No, no,' she said wildly. 'I don't want to go to Nikko. I don't want ever to see him again! I don't want that. You misjudge me, Peter. I only want to be alone — if you have no further use for me.'

He came slowly toward her. In his way he was suffering as badly as Janine. His vanity, his pride were terribly hurt. His disappointment in her was intense. But he still loved her — that was what hurt him most. Suddenly he pulled her on to her feet and with a queer, rough gesture pushed her fair head back against his shoulder and kissed her on the mouth.

'I daresay I shall have — this sort of use for you,' he said, brutally. 'I'm not going to let you go — to let any other poor fool be taken in by your marvellous, innocent eyes. No, Jan, you belong to me and you might as well stay with me. I adored you. I would have kissed your feet last night. Tonight, my dear, I *despise* you!'

'Peter — for God's sake — '

The big, luxurious bedroom seemed to spin about her. She went limp in his arms. He went on kissing her with those fierce, scornful kisses that hurt her so much more than his anger. She felt him lift her on to her bed and put her down against the pillows and after that she knew nothing — because she had fainted.

* * *

There was somebody else playing at Nikko's game of 'pursue your prey'. He had followed Janine to London because he wanted her money. Clare Willington followed Nikko because she happened to still want him for love. Yes, she was still in love with the dancer. Clare possessed a strong streak of perversity in her nature. She wanted what she could not get. Now that Nikko was sick of her and had shown her that it was never herself so much as her money that he had wanted, she was more than ever madly in love with him. She was filled with the most violent desire to get him back and make him her lover again.

So it happened that when Nikko returned to his hotel and marched into his bedroom, he was amazed to find a woman sitting in a chair by the window, smoking a cigarette. Clare, herself.

'What the hell are you doing here?' he asked her.

She stood up, stubbed her cigarette end on an ash tray and came toward him. Her cheeks reddened. But she smiled.

'That isn't a very pretty way to greet the woman you care for, Nikko.'

'I think it's been fairly obvious that I don't care for you — hasn't it?' he asked brutally.

Her flush deepened. The tears sprang to her eyes.

'Nikko, Nikko, be kind to me,' she said in a suffocated voice. 'Nikko, I'm terribly unhappy. I've travelled day and night with only one wish — to get to you — to feel your arms around me again. Nikko, you loved me once. Won't you love me again?'

He stood rigid, unbending. Her passion did not rouse him. It annoyed him. He did not care a hang what Clare Willington suffered. And in a way he hated her. He had committed a crime for her sake. She didn't know it but he had. An unnecessary crime. She hadn't been worth it. And now he was revolted by her and the hideous memory of that revolver shot on the terrace of the Casino.

He unclasped her arms from his neck.

'Get out and leave me in peace. I

hate the sight of you!' he said between his teeth.

She fell back, panting, white to the lips. Then all her thwarted passions culminated into hysteria. She screamed at him — half laughing — half crying.

'You beast! Oh, you beast! To say that to me. To *me* and in Monte you said you adored me — that you would marry me — that you'd give your life to marry me if I were free. Oh, my God, to think that I wanted Derry out of the way — for your sake! Derry — who was always decent to me — who worshipped me — '

'Oh, shut up!' broke in Nikko savagely. 'What the hell's the use of talking about Derry now?'

'No use — he's dead — and it's your fault. You killed him!' screamed Clare, with a face scarlet, distorted with passion.

She meant that it was her *affaire de coeur* with this man which had helped to drive Derry to suicide. But her ill-chosen words had an astonishing effect upon Nikko. She saw his face grow ashen and his jaw drop. His eyes almost bolted out of his head.

'*God!*' he said hoarsely. 'What do you mean . . . what do you know . . . ?'

Then he broke off; choking. He could have bitten his tongue out. He cursed himself for a fool. Of course Clare knew nothing. Was he mad . . . to give himself away like that?

'Young Willington killed himself because he was broke, gambling!' he muttered. 'It had nothing to do with me.'

But it was too late. Clare's hysteria died. What he had said — the way he looked — had roused a fearful suspicion in her. If ever guilt stared out of a man's face it had stared from his; in his protruding eyes and ashen cheeks and gaping mouth. Her unconscious shot had gone home. She suddenly moved back from him and put a finger to her trembling lips.

'Good heavens!' she whispered. 'Nikko — I believe — '

'What — what's the matter?' He jerked at his collar.

'I believe that you *did* kill Derry.'

He went livid again, but he laughed.

'Are you out of your mind?'

'No. But I think I have been — until now. I'm beginning to see light. You wanted me . . . my money . . . and Derrick was in the way. He didn't commit suicide. You . . . '

'Be quiet — you're mad, I say!' broke in Nikko. Terror stared starkly from his gleaming eyes.

Clare gave him another searching look. Then she stared round her, as though hunted, pursued by demons. She gave a piercing cry.

'You murdered him — *murdered my husband!*'

Nikko took a step toward her.

'Clare — in heaven's name — be quiet — you're crazy — it's a lie — '

But she stooped, picked up her hat and fled from the room. He rushed after her, but she had gone, down the stairs . . . out of the hotel.

* * *

Janine and Peter had just finished a miserable meal that evening when a servant announced that Mrs. Derrick Willington had called and wished to see Mr. Willington on urgent business.

Peter looked at his wife. She was very pale. She looked both ill and unhappy. There were blue shadows under her eyes; a little twist of pain to her lips.

When she had recovered from her fainting fit she had found herself alone in her bedroom, but Peter had left a note on her pillow. In cold, curt terms, he had informed her that she must continue to live with him and obey him and that as long as she remained faithful and obedient, he would continue to look upon her as his wife.

An unhappy, humiliating position for Janine. But she had no choice save to accept what he offered. Her whole soul cried out for his love . . . for the exquisite intimacy and happiness which they had known in Paris. But it seemed that it had gone — for ever. This happiness had been a frail, lovely bubble which had burst.

Peter had scarcely spoken to her during dinner and she barely lifted her thick lashes. She did not want him to see the naked pain in her eyes..

The name, Mrs. Derrick Willington, filled her with fresh uneasiness. Why had Clare come? What new trouble was brewing? Janine stayed in the dining-room whilst Peter interviewed his sister-in-law in the sitting-room.

Peter found Clare in a state of excitement and acute nerves.

'I had to see you at once,' she said, pressing a handkerchief to her lips.

'If it is anything important,' said Peter coldly.

'It is — terribly important. It's about Derry.'

Peter stiffened.

'What about him?'

'Sit down — and I'll tell you,' she said, shivering.

She had rushed away from Nikko in

horror. All her love for him had died. She was left with a vindictive desire to punish him — get back on him for what he had done to her, rather than what he had done to Derrick. He had thrown her love back in her face. Very well, Mr. Nikko should pay and pay heavily for that.

'Peter,' said Clare. 'Do you remember telling me in Monte Carlo that you couldn't believe that Derry would take his own life?'

'I do — yes.' Peter winced at the memory of his beloved brother's tragic end.

'Well — I know now that Derry didn't commit suicide.'

Peter stared.

'Are you mad?' he asked her. But his heart jumped in a queer way.

'No. Quite sane. I have my suspicions — very grave suspicions — *that Derry was murdered.*'

Peter whitened. He drew a deep breath.

'Clare! In heaven's name — '

'Yes. I mean it. Derry didn't shoot himself. I believe he was shot — by another's hand.'

For an instant, silence. Peter's blue eyes pierced his sister-in-law's face. He saw that she was not acting. She meant what she said.

'Why are you saying this? What are your reasons for thinking poor old Derry was murdered?' he asked hoarsely.

The desire for revenge had bitten deeply into the woman's soul and she told Peter everything. She disclosed even her sordid passion for Nikko the dancer; their *liaison*; and the scene that had just taken place in Nikko's hotel.

'He took my words literally, Peter. He went green with fright. He asked me what I knew — then tried to back out of it. But I believe that he shot poor Derry, and as God is my judge, Peter, I didn't mean that to happen — no matter how much I wanted my lover.'

Peter clenched his hands. He felt

physically sick. He stared as through a red mist at the pale face of Derrick's widow. Then he said:

'I believe you, Clare,' he said. 'I do believe that although you were unfaithful to my brother — and treated him rottenly — you wouldn't have wished him to die such a hideous death.'

'No — no — I swear it!' she cried and burst into tears.

Peter did not hear her hysterical sobbing. He was thinking of his brother — and of Nikko. That low cur — oh, God, if he had sent Derrick to his death, then he, Peter, would never rest until he had brought him to justice. This thing was only a bare suspicion at the moment. They had no proof — nothing but Clare's word. But somehow, Peter sensed that Clare was right. He would leave no stone unturned to bring this thing to light, now that the seed of suspicion had been sown in his own mind.

Suddenly he turned and walked to the door.

'Wait here, Clare. I wish to see — my wife,' he said.

'Why — what has she to do with it?'

'She was the first one to find Derrick and call for help,' he said strangely. 'And I'm going to ask her a few leading questions.'

He returned to the dining-room where Janine sat in miserable silence.

'Janine,' he said curtly. 'I want you to answer certain questions that I am going to put to you, and I want you to tell me the truth — and nothing but the truth — as though you were a witness in a court of law.'

She caught her breath. His face, his voice frightened her.

'Peter — what is it?'

'Clare has come here with a terrible story — a suspicion that she has imparted to me. She believed that my brother, Derrick, did not commit suicide. She thinks that he was murdered — in cold blood outside the Casino — that he was shot down by another's hand.

Janine stared at her husband. She went scarlet, then white. Then a queer, choking cry escaped her.

'Oh, oh — what am I going to do?'

Peter came up to her and gripped her shoulders. He looked into her eyes.

'Janine — what do *you* know about it? Answer me. It was you who discovered my brother's body. You heard that shot. Are you still quite sure that he shot himself — that not another human being was in sight?'

She tried to answer but no words came. Terror robbed her of the power to speak. She managed, somehow, to gasp a question at her husband.

'Peter — whom do — do you suspect?'

'Whom does Clare suspect, do you mean? Shall I tell you?' . . . Peter's blue eyes flickered dangerously. 'She suspects — and very strongly — *your lover.*'

'Peter — who do you mean?' Janine's voice and eyes were full of horror.

'I mean Nikko, your late dancing partner.'

'Nikko!' echoed Janine. 'But why him?'

Peter's hands dropped from her shoulders.

'Clare has just had a row with him,' he said. 'You'd better know exactly what was said.'

He repeated Clare's story of the scene with Nikko and of the dancer's slip — how his guilty face and manner had given him away.

Janine, deathly white, leaned against the table. She felt sick to the very soul. She stared blindly at Peter. *And she knew* . . . knew the truth — the whole, horrible truth. Of course, Nikko *had* murdered Derrick Willington that night outside the Casino. It had been Nikko whom she had seen vanishing into the bushes — just before she had discovered Derrick's body. Nikko had shot him. And that was why Nikko had married her — and made her promise to say nothing. To keep her mouth shut. To save himself.

'What a dreadful, ghastly mess it all is,' she said in a tragic voice.

'What do you know? What have you to say?' he asked her.

'Only this. I've known all along that your brother didn't kill himself.'

Peter looked down at the beautiful face of his young wife and read the horror, the despair written on it.

'You've known all along? Then, in God's name, why didn't you tell me?'

'I didn't — dare.'

'Didn't dare. Why?'

'I can't explain,' she said, putting both hands to her head. 'I can't . . . '

'You can and shall. Or I'll explain for you,' he broke out, aghast at her duplicity. 'You knew that dancing swine did it. You've been shielding your lover all this time. In other words, you're an accessory after the fact. It's a criminal offence, you know, and — '

She broke in vehemently:

'Peter — it isn't *true!* Nikko isn't my lover in the way you think and I have *not* been shielding him.'

'But you admit you knew that he shot my brother — '

'No — no — I didn't know — I didn't know that it was Nikko!' she denied passionately.

Peter set his teeth.

'Well, I know, now, and by heaven, I'll make him swing for it.'

She put a hand to her lips.

'What are you going to do, Peter?'

'Bring that hound to justice.'

'You can't — you can't, now.'

'I can and shall. I shall drag him back to Monte Carlo and the whole case shall be re-opened. My poor brother was buried as a suicide — coward — our name was dragged in the mud. It was grossly unfair. I tell you, the Willingtons have never been cowards, whatever they've done. He shall be vindicated. The world shall know that he was foully murdered — that he did not take his own life.'

'You can't — prove anything!' whispered Janine.

'You can help me prove it. You saw

that man running away . . . '

He turned on his heel and walked to the door. Then Janine sprang after him, the blood rushing to her white, young face. She caught his arm between her small, cold fingers.

'Peter, listen, don't — don't do anything — please, I implore you not to.'

She was pleading for him as well as for herself. She saw awful visions of the terrible scandal which would evolve from this thing. Her name would be linked with Nikko's — and she was Peter Willington's wife. She might be condemned with Nikko — made an accessory after the fact. She did not care what they did to her. She was past caring. Nothing mattered to her if Peter had stopped caring for her. But there was his name — that name which was now also hers.

'Peter — for your own sake — leave things alone and don't be dragged into the scandal!' she implored.

He hesitated. Then he shook off her

desperate fingers.

'You're very anxious to save Mr. Nikko, aren't you?'

He walked out of the room and shut the door. He deliberately shut out the sight of his young wife's ravaged face and the sound of her agonized crying.

He went back to his sister-in-law.

'Clare — something that my wife has told me convinces me that you are right about this man, Nikko. He shall swing for it — if he is, as we think — Derry's murderer.'

Clare shivered.

'Yes — it's only just,' she said.

And she thought, savagely:

'You let me down — you humiliated me — it's your own fault, Nikko, if I've betrayed you now.'

'Where is the fellow to be found?' came Peter's voice. It sounded tired. His face was fine-drawn and very weary and his eyes were strained.

'I followed him,' said Clare, 'and found him staying at a hotel — near Victoria Street.'

'I'll go there at once.'

'He may have left. He said he was leaving.'

Peter clicked his tongue against his teeth.

'Yes, there's that possibility. But I've got money and we can employ private detectives. We'll trace him.'

Clare considered this a moment. Then a cunning look came into her eyes. She was no more concerned with bringing her late husband's murderer to justice than with the settlement of her multitudinous bills. She drew nearer Peter. With a hypocritical little sob she pressed a handkerchief to her eyes.

'Peter — will you believe how truly and deeply I regret my unkindness to Derry and my mad passion for that fiend — Nikko? I was off my head. I'll do everything on earth now to help you and avenge poor Derry.'

Peter was ready to believe her. He was so unhappy about his wife and the whole beastly business; he was only too willing to snatch at a straw of comfort.

It was some comfort to know that Derrick's widow was going to play the game at last. She looked ghastly, poor woman. He patted her hand.

'All right, Clare — buck up. We're both of us in this and we'll stick together. Where are you staying?'

'I — did mean to stay at Cartman's — ' she let her head sink with a pretty show of distress. 'But now . . . no, no — I want to blot out the memory of Nikko. Where shall I go? What shall I do? I'm in such dreadful straits financially . . . '

Peter drew a cheque-book from his pocket. He forgot that he had once mistrusted this woman. He told himself that he must be decent to Derry's widow and look after her. Derry wouldn't have liked to see his beautiful, luxury-loving wife on her beam-ends in London. Peter wrote her a generous cheque.

She departed, profuse with her thanks and her apologies for past mistakes. Peter sighed wearily after she had gone. Was she genuine or not? He did not really know. But what did it matter? He had lost Janine. All hopes of happiness down at Lullion House, of that sweet domesticity with her as his wife and mother of his children — were dead and buried. Nothing was left but bitterness and the desire to avenge Derrick.

He took a taxi to the hotel. But the bird had flown. The manager of the Cartman informed him that the gentleman who was there under the name of Monsieur Nicholas from Monte Carlo — had gone.

'Without paying his bill, too,' said the man angrily. 'I'd like to find him. Wrong 'un, isn't he?'

'Yes,' said Peter curtly. He was disappointed to find that Nikko had got away. It meant trouble! He left the hotel and went straight to an expensive firm of private-detectives with a reputation for smart work. He engaged two men to trace Nikko, the well-known exhibition dancer, at once.

'He shouldn't be hard to find. He's 'broke' and he'll have to apply for work at one of the hotels,' Peter informed the two men. 'And it'll be easy to stop him if he tries to get abroad. Understand that at the moment I want the affair absolutely private.'

It was fairly late when he returned to his flat. He had had no dinner. He felt ill and tired. He did not see Janine when he got in. He did not bother to look for her. He felt absolutely worn out, and too depressed to care about anything.

Early next morning he received an urgent telephone call from the private detective agency.

'We have traced your dancer, Nikko,' he was told. 'It was not difficult. We found the taxi-cab that drove him from the hotel. He is in lodgings, under the name of Monsieur Nicholas, in a street off Russell Square.'

Peter — with a grim look in his eyes — took down the address and marched out. His own car and chauffeur were waiting for him. He drove rapidly to the lodgings where Nikko was in hiding.

Nikko, never dreaming that detectives had 'shadowed him', was amazed and terrified when — while he sat eating his breakfast in the shabby sitting-room of his 'digs' — Peter Willington walked in and interrupted him.

He let his knife and fork fall to the plate with a clatter and sprang up — white as the table-napkin which he raised to his lips. The dancer was beside himself with terror. He stared at the face of Derrick Willington's brother — a relentless, powerful face — with vengeance written in the hard, blue eyes. Nikko's blood seemed to turn to water within his veins. He felt deathly sick. But he tried to laugh — the laugh of a desperate man.

'Why this charming visit, Mr. Willington?'

'I have come with only one object,' said Peter in a voice as grim as his eyes. 'I want to tell you that I know you murdered my brother, Derrick, on the terrace outside the Casino in Monte Carlo one month ago.'

The room spun round Nikko. His dark, distended eyes stared at the other man and his face went green. He hung on to the back of his chair for support.

'Do you deny the murder?' came Peter's cold voice.

'I — yes — good God — I — ' Nikko stuttered and choked for breath.

'I think not,' said Peter. 'You can't deny it. You shot my brother in cold blood, as he came out of the Casino. My sister-in-law knows it. *My wife knows it*. You can't deny it and you will come with me, now, to the police and make your confession.'

Nikko's knees shook under him . . . sagged. He put a hand to his throat as though already he felt a rope choking him. It was beyond him now to deny the truth. Peter seemed to know too much. And Clare had betrayed him, had she? Well — there was always Janine to use as a lever.

'One moment,' said Nikko. 'Perhaps you won't appear quite so keen to hand me over to the law when you hear one or two things about Janine that you don't know now.'

'About Janine!' repeated Peter sharply. 'What do you mean?'

Nikko licked his dry lips.

'I mean this. If you persist in hounding me — in having me arrested — I should tell the world what you don't happen to know. That Janine is a *bigamist*.'

Peter blinked his eyes.

'A bigamist?' he repeated slowly. 'What are you talking about?'

'What I say. Jan had no right to marry you. She was already married — to me.'

If the man had flung a bombshell at Peter Willington's feet and it had exploded, then and there, it could not have caused a more terrific upheaval for Peter. Stupefied, he looked from his great height down into the dark, glittering eyes of the dancer. His brain seemed like cotton-wool — incapable of clear thought. But gradually there sank into it these words . . . 'Jan was already married — to me!' *Already married . . . to Nikko*.

Peter broke out in a violent voice:

'That's a damned lie.'

'It's the truth. She married me in the Chapel of St. Therese, in the mountains at the back of Monte . . . and here is the certificate which I am keeping for her — with our names — the date — the signatures of our witnesses . . . '

With shaking fingers, Nikko opened a despatch case, drew out a document and handed it to Peter who — still stupefied — looked at it — read every word written upon it. Yes, it seemed in order. A correct marriage certificate — signed by the priest, the witnesses, and lastly by the bride and groom. There was Jan's name. Janine O'Mara — the maiden name she had signed when she had married him, Peter.

It hit Peter to the depths of his being — and hit him hard. He suddenly looked for a chair, sat down heavily and put his head between his hands.

'Oh, my God!' he said.

Nikko looked on without pity. He had no use for this high-principled young man and no compassion for his griefs. He only wanted to save his own neck.

'You see, Willington,' he said, 'if you persist in making this affair public, you'll drag up all the dirty details. It'll come out in court that Janine is a bigamist and an accessory after the crime. You'll hang me — but you'll land her in gaol as well. Do you want to see her serving a term in Holloway?'

Peter raised bloodshot eyes to the other man.

'God knows what I ought to do,' he said.

Nikko came nearer him — touched his arm.

'Willington — let us both go. It can't make things better for you.'

'No — it can only clear my brother's name.'

'Let us go, man. Wipe it out.'

Peter gave a hollow laugh.

'Wipe it out! How impossible that is!'

Could anything ever blot out the fact that Janine had lived with him as his wife and he had taken her in his arms as a lover and worshipped her and believed in her love for him.

With great bitterness Peter reviewed the situation. But he blamed himself as well as Janine. He should never have married her or allowed himself to be so fooled. He must reproach his own folly as well as her sin. She was obviously a weak, foolish girl — still a mere child — infatuated with this man, Nikko, and led by him to her ruin.

A red mist suddenly came before Peter's eyes. His blood flared up in fierce rebellion, in the thirst for vengeance.

'You can go,' he said through clenched teeth. 'You can quit — the pair of you. For the girl's sake I'll let you off lightly. But first of all, you filthy hound, take this . . . before I leave here.'

He sprang and smashed his fist between the dancer's eyes. It was a knock-out blow. Nikko went down like a ninepin and crumpled up on the floor. Like one drunk, Peter Willington turned and stumbled out of the room. He left Nikko lying there.

* * *

When Nikko recovered from that knock-out blow which Peter had given him, he was a very sorry figure. The perfect, cameo-like face was bruised and swollen. There was an abrasion between his eyes where Peter's knuckles had torn the flesh. It gave his features an ugly menacing appearance. His head was splitting with pain.

He knew, however, that he must pull himself together. He was in a tight corner. Willington had abandoned the effort to bring him to justice. But there was still Clare to be reckoned with. He must see her — win her back and so assure his own safety.

Nikko bathed his injured face; put a piece of sticking plaster between his eyes and drank a stiff brandy and soda. He cursed Peter Willington. He cursed Janine. He cursed Clare. But he was not going to give up hope and let these people triumph over him.

First he must find Clare. He had no idea where she was but he was cunning and he found out. He went to a telephone-box and rang up Cartman's Hotel. Perhaps Clare had taken a room there. He found that she had not. He hung up the receiver gloomily. Where had she gone? He thought hard for a moment. He remembered, in the days when he had been intimate with Clare, she had told him that she had a woman friend in London — a very great friend with whom she always kept in touch. Now, what was that woman's name? She was rather a well-known Society hostess.

Nikko remembered. Vera Daubeney. Lady Daubeney. He turned over the pages of the telephone directory feverishly. Daubeney . . . Lady Vera. There it was. He got on to the number. A maid answered. He asked to speak to her ladyship. The maid answered that her ladyship was abroad — she had left for Norway, that morning, on a fishing expedition with Sir John. Nikko's heart sank. He said:

'Do you by any chance know where I can find Lady Daubeney's friend — Mrs. Derrick Willington?'

The maid's answer was more successful than Nikko had dared hope.

'Why, yes, sir. Mrs. Willington is here. As a matter of fact her ladyship has lent Mrs. Willington the flat for a month while she is abroad. She moved here this afternoon from the Grosvenor Hotel. Shall I ask Madam to speak to you?'

'No, thanks,' said Nikko. 'And you need not give any message. I'll call — later in the day.'

He went out of the telephone-box, biting nervously at his lips. That was a piece of luck and smart of him to have remembered Lady Daubeney. So Clare had been lent the flat? Nikko had memorised the address from the directory.

It was four o'clock in the afternoon when he boldly put in an appearance at the Mansions. The maid who received him said that Madam had been lying down since lunch but that if he would wait in the drawing-room, she would tell Madam he was here.

'What name shall I give, sir?'

Nikko licked his lips and narrowed his dark, feverish eyes.

'Say Mr. Willington,' he said deliberately.

He was afraid that Clare would not see him if he gave his own name.

Clare, when she imagined that her brother-in-law had called, rose from her bed — dressed rapidly. She put on a primrose chiffon negligée and made herself look particularly charming. She wanted to make herself very pleasant to Peter. He was chancellor of her exchequer. She had telephoned to Peter's flat an hour ago to let him know that she had taken Vera Daubeney's flat for a month. A servant had taken the message and told her Mr. Willington was not in, but Clare fully expected Peter to communicate with her. They were on good terms now.

She felt quite gay and happy when she opened the door of Lady Daubeney's pretty gold and cream drawing-room. Then her expression changed, her whole body stiffened when she saw the man who had come to see her. Amazed and furious she stared at him. Nikko. How *dared* he?

He advanced toward her nervously. He looked humble, almost servile.

'Clare — I had to come — I went to a lot of trouble to find you,' he began huskily.

'Why?'

Her voice was not encouraging. He licked his lips.

'Clare — we've had a little misunderstanding. I'm damned sorry for behaving like a cad. I was off my head with worry — financial worry. I regret it bitterly and I've come to ask you to wipe out our last few meetings and begin again — where we left off in Monte Carlo.'

She was silent. But she looked at him dangerously. So he had come to whine, had he? Got the wind up, perhaps. Reaction had set in with Clare. Her passion for this man had changed to malicious dislike. Never while she lived would she forgive or forget his treatment of her — his repulse of her advances at Cartman's Hotel.

'So you've come here to say you're sorry, have you, Nikko?' she said, in a silky voice.

'*Mon Dieu*, but I *am* sorry,' he broke out in a passionate voice. 'You must try and understand — I've been crazy with worry. I didn't want a woman in my life — I couldn't afford to give you all the beautiful things you deserved and I thought it better to end our affair. But now I realize how much I care for you.

I can't live without you. I had to come back, Clare, *ma mie!*'

He drew nearer — so near that she could feel his breath on her cheeks. She drew back a pace.

'And what about — my husband — whom you murdered?' she asked in her sweetest voice.

He started violently and changed colour.

'Clare — that ridiculous tale! You were mad in the hotel. You know perfectly well I didn't shoot Willington,' he began to stutter. 'Good God — you can't be serious about that. You know it isn't true.'

'You didn't shoot him? And you still love me. You've come here to tell me those two things?' Clare's voice was still silken. Nikko was too agitated to hear the knife-edge behind it.

'Yes, I've come here to tell you that I'm absolutely innocent of that horrible crime, and that I do still love you,' he said eagerly. 'Clare — *cherie* — let us begin again — let us be lovers — as we were at the Etoile. Ah, darling, I'm hungry for your lips — I want your tender arms about me. I've suffered terribly.'

She smiled. It was a cruel smile but he took heart from it. He caught her in his arms.

'There isn't another woman on earth to compare with you, Clare,' he said.

He was sincere about this love-making. He very much wanted Clare's love again. He needed the comfort of it. The assurance that she no longer suspected him of her husband's murder.

'Clare — kiss me — show me that you love me still,' he said huskily.

Then, suddenly, startling him, she tore herself out of his embrace, flung back her head and laughed loudly Laughed and laughed, until Nikko stared — wondering if she were crazy.

'Clare!' he protested.

'You fool!' she said, in a low, venomous tone. 'You poor fool! Do you think I believe one word you say? Do you really deceive yourself that I'm going to accept you as my lover and believe that you are innocent? No! I know you're guilty — guilty of my poor Derry's murder and you're going *to be hanged for it*.'

Nikko stepped back, ashen to the lips.

'Clare — in God's name!'

'You murdered Derry!' she continued in a high, shrill voice. 'Then you turned round and deserted me because I lost my money — insulted me. You did that — and you expect me to love and comfort you? No, Nikko. You made me suffer badly, but now you're going to suffer much more than I did.'

She darted to a side-table where there was a telephone under a brocaded doll. She lifted the doll and picked up the receiver. Her eyes — brilliant, malicious, glittered at Nikko.

'I'm going to get on to the police station,' she said.

4

The butler-valet in charge of Peter's service-flat brought Janine lunch. At the same time he gave her a message.

'I took it on the telephone, madam. I thought you were resting, so I did not disturb you. From Mrs. Derrick Willington. Her telephone number is Park Drive 8000.'

Janine took the piece of paper which the man handed her and folded it listlessly. She said:

'Thank you!'

But she hardly saw the servant, neither did she touch the food he brought her. She stared out of the window with heavy eyes grown tired and sore with weeping. Her heart beat slowly. She was in the very depths of depression. Peter had been gone some hours. So far as Janine was concerned they might have been years.

Then, as the moments dragged by, she began to concentrate on the telephone message, which the butler had just given her. Clare's address. Clare was Peter's sister-in-law. She had been here to see Peter. They were friendly just now. No doubt Clare would know where to find Peter. Janine sprang to her feet. Her eyes glittered in her white, young face.

'I must find him,' she thought.

She darted to her bedroom, put on a coat and hat and hurried from the flat. Downstairs, she called a page.

'Taxi, at once . . . '

'Yes, madam,' said the boy, and hastened to do her bidding.

Janine stood on the steps of the entrance. The warm sun touched her softly, but she shivered as though an icy wind was blowing. Every nerve in her body was jarred. It was all she could do to keep her teeth from chattering.

The taxi drew up. Janine stepped into it and gave the address of the flat wherein Clare was staying.

She did not see what streets they drove through. Her wide eyes stared blindly from the windows. She only knew that in a very short time the car drew up before a new white block of flats near Hyde Park Corner, and the taxi-man opened the door and said:

' 'Ere you are, miss . . . '

She stepped out automatically and paid him double his fare. She did not wait for change. She walked into the building and the lift-boy took her up. He glanced at her once or twice. He had never seen a more beautiful young lady than this one with her fair hair, her exquisite features and slim, graceful figure. But there was something almost terrifying about the expression in her wide eyes — and the ashen pallor of her cheeks. She looked very ill, poor young lady, he thought, and — as he afterwards remarked to a fellow worker: 'Like as she'd 'ad a shock!'

They reached Lady Daubeney's front door. The lift-boy rang the bell for her. Nobody answered. A maid — the girl who waited on this particular flat — passed by with a tray in her hands. She paused as she saw Janine.

'Mrs. Willington's just gone out, miss . . . '

'Gone out! Are you sure?' asked Janine.

'Yes, miss. I saw her go down. But perhaps you'd like to wait . . . '

'I would,' said Janine.

The maid, holding her tray in one hand, took a key from her belt and fitted it in the lock of the front door.

'If you don't mind going in and sitting down, I'll let madam know as soon as she comes back.'

Janine pushed open the door and walked in. The moment she was inside that flat she was struck by a feeling of chill, of terror. And she *knew* instinctively that all was not well here. She did not know why but she began to tremble violently, as she walked down the unfamiliar hall which was beautifully and expensively decorated and furnished.

She pushed open a door and saw an empty bedroom. She opened another door. Then she clapped both hands to her mouth to stifle a scream.

'Oh, my God — Nikko!' she whispered.

And she knew why she had been frightened; why she had felt, intuitively, that something terrible had happened here. She had a confused glimpse of a luxurious drawing-room, cream and gold; and a gold-hued carpet. On that carpet, sprawling in a grotesque and sinister attitude, was a man. His face was turned from her. But Janine knew who it was. She knew the graceful lines of that slimly-built body, and that blue-black hair. Nikko. *Nikko* . . . and there was a dark red pool soaking into the gold carpet beside him — an ever-widening pool. She turned him over, fighting down hysteria.

'Nikko . . . Nikko!'

His head lolled back as she rolled him. She saw a face that was waxen white, the lips open, dolorously. But his eyes were shut and not open and staring, so she knew he was not dead. Her terrified gaze sped to a rent in his coat, just by his heart, and saw a crimson rivulet of blood welling from it. On the carpet lay a small, bright automatic. The room was acrid yet with the odour of smoke.

'Nikko,' Janine called his name frantically. She seized his left hand and chafed it desperately.

'Nikko . . . '

The hand was very cold and clammy and there was no response from the fingers that she held. Then his black, thick lashes lifted, slowly, heavily. She saw his eyes — dark, opaque, agonized. They looked up into hers, saw and recognized.

'Jan!' he whispered.

'Nikko, in God's name what has happened?'

The thick lashes flickered. The pale lips twisted into a smile that was a grimace. And now a little strength came back to him. His fingers gripped her hand.

'Clare . . . did me . . . in . . . '

'You mean she shot you?'

'Yes. We quarrelled . . . ' His voice was so faint she could only just catch what he said. 'She threatened to give me up . . . police . . . I tried to . . . stop her . . . She found my revolver and . . . shot me . . . or maybe . . . it . . . just . . . went off . . .

Janine looked round her in a bewildered way.

'I must get help. You must be attended to — oh, heavens — !'

'No good . . . got me through . . . lung,' he whispered. 'Jan . . . listen . . . I . . . behaved . . . damnably to you. Want to . . . make amends . . . Find a piece of paper — quickly — it's getting so . . . damned dark . . . '

The room was brilliant with sunlight. But to him it was dark. Janine shuddered. She found a piece of paper on the writing-bureau in front of the windows and a fountain-pen. Nikko lay still, closed eyes, breathing stertoriously. Terrible, laboured breathing that filled Janine with horror, for she realized that she was alone here with a dying man.

She put an arm about him and raised him. He groaned terribly but managed to take the pen between his fingers. It was a supreme effort on his part. His eyes were filming as he signed that name 'Nikko', for the last time on this earth. Then the pen dropped from his nerveless hand. He whispered:

'Sorry . . . Jan . . . '

His head fell back and Janine knew that she held a dead man in her arms.

She let him drop back on the carpet and stood up, shuddering: the fair hair clung damply to her wet forehead. She could no longer look at Nikko. He was not good to look at. She folded that pathetic confession which he had signed and put it in her bag. She looked this way and that, wondering what to do now and where to go. She put a hand to her eyes.

Suddenly her nerve went. She ran to the doorway — panting — sobbing . . . distraught. But a man's figure blocked the doorway; a tall, athletic figure. She ran straight into it and drew back. She looked up into a pair of stern blue eyes — felt two firm hands grip her shoulders.

'Janine!' said a deep voice. 'For God's sake, what have you done?'

She grew quiet. She recognized Peter, her husband. She knew not whether she was relieved or aghast. But she turned and pointed speechlessly to Nikko's body.

'Yes,' said Peter. 'I know. You killed him. You had a quarrel and you shot him. I understand.'

His face was grim and very tired. He had come here to see Derrick's widow — talk over the future with her. He had meant to settle a little money on her — for Derry's sake. And he had decided to let his brother's murderer go free, rather than put Jan into prison and make her suffer.

Now he came face to face with her again. In the most terrible way, under the most unexpected circumstances. He had found the front door of this flat open and walked in. The first thing he had seen when he reached the drawing-room was the body of Nikko, the dancer, on the floor. One look at the white face and staring eyes had told Peter that the man was dead. Then Janine — blind with terror — had run into his arms. He took it for granted that she had shot 'her husband' during a quarrel with him and was trying to escape from the scene of her crime.

Janine found her voice.

'Peter — I — didn't — do it — '

'My dear child, of course you did it. I can see that. There's nobody else here — but you two. It's so obvious. A quarrel — and this end. Don't trouble to deny it. Own up and let me help you . . . '

Janine tried to speak again — to ward off this new horror. But her head reeled and the gold and white room was spinning about her.

'Janine — pull yourself together,' said Peter's voice — still very calm.

Then she laughed hysterically and pitched forward into his arms.

* * *

When Clare fled from Lady Daubeney's flat she took it for granted that Nikko would recover. It never entered her head that he would die. They had fought and struggled. The revolver which she had found in his pocket had gone off. She had never meant it to go off. But of course it had not killed him. She would send a doctor to him at once. She decided not to let anybody in the block know, because of the scandal. She walked from the building in Park Drive to the nearest post office. She found a doctor's name and number — a West End doctor — and called him up.

When she came out of that post office, panic seized her. It occurred to her for the first time that Nikko might not recover. She did not know whether to go back or whether to vanish. No — that would at once suggest that she was guilty. Clare's teeth chattered. Not a pleasant thought — that she might be arrested for murder or at least for manslaughter. She walked down street after street — trying to make up her mind what to do. She walked for fully an hour before she made the decision to return to the flat and face it out.

Meanwhile, Dr. Fuller, the physician to whom she had telephoned, had come to the conclusion that there was something 'fishy' about that hysterical call for aid from the Park Drive post office telephone-box. He was a young man, just making a good reputation and anxious not to get mixed up in any scandals without doing the correct and proper thing. He took a policeman with him when he went to No. 24, Park Drive Mansions — to be on the safe side.

Dr. Fuller and the policeman reached

the flat very soon after Peter Willington reached it. Peter heard them coming. He was still sitting beside Janine — trying to bring her back to consciousness. His heart sank and his lips tightened grimly when he heard the voices of the two men in the hall.

'Now we're done!' he thought.

Janine's long lashes lifted. Her eyes opened.

'Peter!' she whispered.

'Get up,' he whispered back. 'Get up and for God's sake keep quiet — don't say a word. They're here . . . '

'Who?' She stammered — terror crowding upon her as full consciousness returned.

'The police,' he said.

'Police. *Peter* . . . '

'Yes. Keep quiet — leave it to me . . . '

He walked out of the room. She struggled on to her feet, pushing the wet gold hair back from her face. She heard Peter's voice:

'Yes, this way. Yes — come in, officer.

There has been an accident — and a fatal one. I'm responsible . . . '

Janine rushed forward, crying out hysterically:

'It wasn't you, Peter — you can't say it was you. You didn't do it and I didn't do it, either.'

'Take no notice of her, officer,' broke in Peter. 'She's not responsible for what she says.'

Janine gave a shrill cry.

'Peter — I didn't do it — '

'No, no, of course you didn't,' he said. 'I did . . . '

'But you didn't!' she began in a frenzied voice. 'Because I know . . . '

'One moment,' interrupted the constable. 'Just one moment, please, miss. Is the gentleman dead, doctor?'

Dr. Fuller, a little pale, unused to dramas of this kind, stood up and wiped his forehead with a large pocket handkerchief.

'Quite dead!' he said. 'He was shot through the right lung.'

The policeman wrote carefully in his

book. Then he turned to Peter.

'Now then, sir — you say you shot the deceased. You'd better come along with me . . . '

'I'm quite ready,' said Peter, quietly.

Janine put both hands to her head. It was as though a dozen hammers beat against her brain. She seemed to hear her own voice from a long distance:

'No, no, *no* . . . . Peter you didn't do it . . . I didn't!'

Then Peter's voice, very calm; rather grim:

'Let's get on with it, officer.'

Janine could scarcely see. Her body shook and her legs were weak and trembling as though she had been very ill for a long time. She ceased to cry out or protest. She looked as though fascinated at the body of Nikko the dancer — that once lithe, graceful, vital body — lay terribly still under a rug which the doctor had put across it.

Peter passed her and gave her a

quick, almost compassionate look.

'Go and lie down. You look ill,' he said.

Suddenly she caught his arm with both her hands.

'But, Peter, wait!' She tried to stammer.

'Come along, please, sir,' came the sharp voice of the policeman.

'Good-bye, Jan,' said Peter. And turned and walked away. He had to unclasp her clinging fingers before he did so. He felt very sick at heart. He followed the policeman out of the room.

Janine began to run after him.

'Peter, come back — listen — Peter — '

Her voice trailed away. She could walk no further. That awful feeling of faintness; of weakness overcame her. She found a chair and sank into it. She wanted to follow Peter and explain. But she could not move.

Dr. Fuller who had come with the policeman — thoroughly glad now that he had brought a member of the law

— saw Janine sitting in the dining-room with her head lolling back and his professional eye at once noted the fact that she was ill. He hurried to her.

'Is there anything I can do for you?' he asked.

Two of the loveliest eyes he had ever seen — quite green between long, dark lashes — opened and looked into his. They were full of unbearable agony.

'Help me . . . ' she whispered. 'Help me . . . please . . . '

He took her wrist and felt her pulse anxiously. He did not like the look of this young woman. She was in a state of collapse. This business had been a shock . . . Of course . . . she was connected with the ghastly affair. Who was she?

'Let me take you home,' he said.

'No — to — the police station.'

'You can't go there — you're not fit — '

'I — must,' she panted. 'Must tell . . . what I know . . . '

'I assure you — ' began Fuller, and

then stopped. The girl's beautiful golden head had dropped forward. He put an arm about her and half lifted, half dragged her to a bed in the next room. So the collapse had come. Complete and utter. She would not be able to move, to speak, to do anything for hours — perhaps for days.

Dr. Fuller reflected. She could not be left alone. The constable was sending in two men and the law had already taken possession of this flat and its sinister, silent occupant. A murder had been committed here. Nothing must be touched. The door would shortly be shut and sealed.

'An ambulance and the hospital,' said the young doctor to himself. 'The only thing. I don't know her address . . . ' He hurried into the hall to the telephone.

It was late that night when Janine came back to her senses. It took her a long time to realize where she was. She found herself in a narrow white bed with the clothes drawn up to her chin

. . . not a crease anywhere. There was a screen round her bed. Dim lights, a sensation that this was a big room; a big building, and the faint odour of antiseptics.

Then she started up wildly. The blood rushed to her cheeks. Her heart beat at a frightful rate. She remembered everything. The murder of Nikko . . . and Peter being taken to the police station. Janine screamed:

'Peter — Peter!'

A white-capped nurse who was standing in the middle of the ward, talking to another nurse, glanced in the direction of the screen.

'Hello — there's No. 22 waking up . . . '

'Peter!' screamed Janine.

'Ssh . . . sssh . . . you're all right,' said the nurse. She reached No. 22's bedside and forced her gently back on the pillow. 'Quiet, my dear — you're all right!'

Janine's eyes stared wildly up at the nurse.

'I must go — I must get to the police station.'

'Ssh — later — not now. It's the middle of the night, my dear, and you've been very ill. You must be quiet.'

Janine lay back on the pillow, panting, exhausted, her brief spark of vitality extinguished. A low moan broke from her.

'Oh, Peter!'

The nurse glanced at her card.

'We want your name and address, please. Can you give it?'

Janine whispered.

'Yes. I am — Mrs. Peter Willington — from — from — '

Her voice died away . . . her eyes closed. The nurse felt for her pulse and let the limp hand drop back on the bed.

'H'm,' she said to herself. 'Lady all right and pretty as a picture, but in a bad state, poor thing. I'd better ask Sister if we can give oxygen . . . '

A cylinder was brought and placed at the bedside of No. 22. Two nurses worked on Janine.

'Mrs. Peter Willington she says her name is, Sister,' said the younger nurse.

'Good heavens alive!' exclaimed the Sister, and stared eagerly at Janine. 'Do you realize who she is?'

'No — who?'

'See the *Evening News?*'

'No.'

'Well, a Mr. Peter Willington has been arrested for murder — shooting some dancer-fellow in a West End flat. This is his wife.'

'I say, what a thrill!' exclaimed the young nurse.

Janine became the centre of interest in the woman's ward that night. When she opened her eyes again she was so feeble that she could barely whisper. She had even ceased to worry about Peter. She was worse before the grey dawn broke over the big hospital at Hyde Park Corner to which she had been taken and it needed all the skill of the house-physician and the nurses to keep her alive. The shock and strain had been too much for Janine.

She had had more than she could bear.

* * *

Clare Willington stole back to Lady Daubeney's flat when it was dark, that same evening. She was exhausted and scared but she decided to go back and see what had happened. She could tramp the streets no longer. She found the big block of flats seething with excitement. Crowds outside the front entrance. Policemen everywhere and a queer atmosphere brooding over everything.

Clare's heart seemed to stop beating when she saw all this. She knew, only too well, what had happened. Nikko was dead. He had been found dead. Heavens, what a frightful thing. *She had killed him!* With a white face and a sick feeling in her heart, she approached the head-porter.

'What has happened?' she stammered.

He looked at her with some excitement.

'Oh, Madam, there's a gentleman from police headquarters been waiting to see you for a long time. Something happened in her ladyship's flat — after you went out. Something terrible . . . '

Clare passed a tongue over her dry lips.

'What happened — good God — what?'

'The gentleman whom you saw up there just before you went out, Madam — was *murdered*,' said the porter, relishing the dramatic announcement.

Clare clenched both her hands. She knew she must look ghastly, but she was thankful that she was wearing a hat; a big summer-straw with a dropping brim, which hid her eyes.

'Murdered . . . ' she repeated faintly. 'Oh, good heavens . . . but by *whom?*'

His answer was totally unexpected.

'A gentleman named Willington — some relative of yours, isn't he, madam? He called here soon after you went out.

He must have quarrelled with the other gentleman. He confesses to having shot him.'

Clare stared blindly and incredulously at the porter. Was he mad — or was she? A gentleman named Willington had confessed to shooting Nikko! It could only be Peter. But why had *he* confessed? Why, in heaven's name? She put a hand to her spinning head. A man in plain clothes approached her.

'Mrs. Derrick Willington?'

'Yes,' she whispered.

'Ah — we've been wanting to see you. I'm from Police H.Q. I want you to answer a few questions, Mrs. Willington . . . '

'Yes,' said Clare, as though she were stunned.

'This way, please,' he said with a sharp look at her. His experienced eye was quick to note that she was trembling violently, and livid save for the vivid artificial scarlet of her lips.

He interviewed her in a small room which was the estate-office of the flats.

'As you have probably been informed, Mrs. Willington, a murder was committed in your flat — the flat Lady Daubeney lent you — shortly after you left it, this afternoon,' he said.

Clare dropped into a chair. She took a handkerchief from her bag and pressed it to her lips. She felt so terribly sick. Nikko was dead . . . *dead*. She was trying to visualize it. She had once loved him madly . . . and he was dead and she had shot him. She recalled his panic-stricken face and the amazed look in his dark eyes as he fell — after she had fired that fatal shot. The detective was questioning her.

'What time did you leave the flat, Mrs. Willington?'

'I think it was about — half-past three,' she said, struggling for composure.

'You left the deceased in the drawing-room..'

'Yes . . . '

'For any particular reason?'

'I — he — wanted to pass away a few hours . . . and I — said he could stay there. I had — an appointment . . . ' Clare lied wildly — the first lies that came into her head.

'An appointment with whom?'

'A friend.'

'I see. That's quite all right, Mrs. Willington. You went out to meet a friend. You have just returned.'

'Yes.'

The detective wrote on a pad.

'Soon after you left,' he said, 'your maid who works in your suite came up with tea for another suite and let a lady into the flat.'

'A — lady?' repeated Clare.

'Yes. A lady whom we believe to be Mrs. Peter Willington.'

'Oh, God — Janine!' thought Clare. 'She must have found Nikko. How frightful . . . '

'And shortly after that,' added the man, 'Mr. Willington was shown up. Presumably there was a difference of opinion between the three of them.

Anyhow, Mr. Willington confesses that he shot this dancer, Nikko, or Mr. Nicholas — whatever his real name was.'

Clare shut her eyes. She breathed spasmodically. So Janine and Peter between them had found Nikko, and Nikko had died. But why, why had Peter taken the blame? That defeated her.

'Rather a shock for you,' said the detective quite kindly.

She looked at him with dilated eyes.

'Where is — Mrs. Peter Willington?'

'She collapsed and was taken to hospital.'

'I see. And Peter . . . my brother-in-law . . . '

'Is in custody . . . at Bow Street.'

Clare hid her ghastly face in her hands. She was swimming in a veritable sea of confusion and perplexity. Terror — horror of the thing she had done held her in a thrall. She had killed Nikko and he was dead. But she hadn't meant to. The automatic had gone off.

She hadn't even known it was loaded. She had just been struggling — dived a hand into Nikko's coat pocket and pulled the thing out . . .

The detective's voice said, gently:

'I'm afraid you can't go back into your flat. It's shut and sealed. But your maid packed your luggage and it's down here in the hall. You'd like to go to an hotel?'

'Yes,' she whispered, trying to control herself. She thought:

'I ought to tell this man now — right away — that I did it. That I'm guilty. But I daren't. I daren't!'

The detective, watching her closely, recognized signs of hysteria; and something more. Fear? He pursed his lips.

'H'm. What's she had to do with all this? She'll need close watching . . . '

Clare staggered somehow or other to the taxi which they called for her. She had told them all she could — and they let her go. She would, they said, be wanted as a witness when Peter Willington came up before the magistrates and at the inquest on Nikko, tomorrow. Feeling deadly ill and frightened, Clare drove away from the Mansions. She knew quite well that she would be watched and that there would be no chance of escape for her. She went to an hotel in Piccadilly and tried to steady her nerves with a brandy and soda and some food.

She did not sleep that night. All night long she alternated between pacing her room and lying on the bed, with aching, staring eyes. Conscience tugged at her . . . tugged and haunted all through those hours. She could not escape from the memory of Nikko's face . . . when he crumpled up at her feet after that shot. She had killed a man.

When morning came, Clare was a haggard wreck. Every nerve was on edge; all traces of good looks wiped away. She looked quite old. She decided to see Janine. She might not be allowed to see Peter but she could find out the truth from Janine.

She drove to the hospital as soon as she was up and dressed. She was, at first, refused admittance. Mrs. Peter Willington was seriously ill — on the danger list. Then Clare pressed her case. She was Mrs. Derrick Willington and she must see Janine. It was of vital importance. Finally she was taken to Janine's bedside and told that she could only stay for a few seconds and that she must not distress the patient, who was in a very grave condition.

Clare sat down beside Peter's young wife. She found the lovely young dancer unbelievably altered. She lay thin, white and lifeless, her eyes closed — black lashes curving against the pallor of cheeks that had hollowed pathetically. The fair hair lay in bright thick plaits on either side of the mask-like face.

'Janine,' she said. 'Janine . . . do you know me? Can you speak to me — just one moment?'

Janine's heavy lashes lifted. She came back from a dark, shadowy world in which she felt she had been drifting out on the tide — to other things — other worlds. She was too tired and too badly hurt to bear any more pain. But she forced herself back when she saw and recognized Derrick Willington's widow. All her fears, her wild terrors for Peter came back. She started up, her face colouring violently.

'Peter!' she gasped. 'Mrs. — Willington — you must save — Peter. He didn't shoot Nikko. I didn't . . . and . . . you know . . . '

'Oh, hush!' broke in Clare, her face ashen. She bent over Janine and put a hand against her lips. 'Ssh . . . don't let others hear. Listen . . . I know nothing . . . tell me . . . '

Janine looked up at her and remembered everything, now.

'You do know,' she whispered. '*You shot Nikko*. He told me so . . . before he died!'

Clare put a hand to her lips. She was trembling from head to foot.

'My God . . . you know! He was alive . . . when you got there? . . . '

'Yes . . . '

'Then why did Peter . . . ?'

'Peter thinks — I did it.'

Janine gasped out the words, and her eyes closed again. Two great tears forced themselves through the dark fringe of lashes and rolled down her hollow cheeks. Clare bowed her head. She understood. Peter thought that his wife had killed Nikko and he had shouldered the blame to save her. He loved her . . . like that.

Janine opened her eyes again.

'Save Peter . . . oh — you can!' she whispered brokenly. Clare shuddered violently.

'I must go,' she said.

'Will you save him?' Janine's voice rose to a cry of agony. 'You *must* . . . '

'Ssh,' said Clare. Then she laid a hand on Janine's burning forehead. 'Be quiet. I'll save him.'

Janine sank back on the pillows and gave a long sigh.

'Thank God,' she said.

A nurse led Clare from the ward. She

ought to go straight to the Coroner's Court to attend the inquest on the murdered man. But she could not go. Could not face it. She could not face a trial, either her own — or Peter's. But decided definitely that she must not let Peter suffer on her account. She had done harm enough to poor Derry; she must not add to her sins by ruining Peter as well.

Clare was not all bad. She had been a selfish, reckless, worldly woman. But she had a conscience and that conscience triumphed now. She realized that a great love existed between Peter and his wife. Let them be happy. Her own career was over. Love, money, everything gone. A charge of manslaughter — or murder — would be too much to live through.

* * *

Peter Willington was a very astonished and almost much relieved man when — at the end of that next day he found himself acquitted without a stain upon his character.

He was informed that his sister-in-law, Clare Willington, had committed suicide and left a signed confession, a description of her quarrel and fight with Nikko the dancer and how accidentally she had shot him. This story was corroborated by Mrs. Peter Willington, who had found the dancer still breathing and he had told her a similar story.

Peter had only one thought in his head when he was released. To get away from the whole sordid, terrible business. He felt that he could stand no more. The last shock of Clare's suicide had completely unnerved him. First poor old Derry's death in Monte Carlo. Then Nikko . . . now Clare.

It seemed to Peter that the whole of his small world was red with blood. Filled with the horror of it, all he wanted was to get away. But as soon as he was released from custody he was told that his wife was in hospital and on the danger list. A message was sent to him from the Matron:

'*Mrs. Willington calls for you constantly. Please come at once . . .* '

Peter knew that he could never forgive himself if he failed to answer that summons. And somehow the knowledge that she was desperately ill and calling for him roused all the old protective instinct which had been the first thing which had drawn him to her in Monte Carlo. Little Janine, so lovely, so young, so friendless . . . how could a man forsake her when once he had held her to his heart as wife?

He hurried to the hospital, all bitterness and resentment submerged in a sudden flash of anxiety on her behalf. The old passionate desire to save her filled him.

'She's not my wife — I must try to remember that,' he told himself as he drove along. 'But I will see her once and do what I can for her. Then never again!'

Janine's temperature was rising and alarming the nurses and doctors in charge of 'No. 22.'

'She keeps calling this Peter. He's her husband and I wish he'd come,' said the Sister of the ward.

A probationer sitting beside Janine glanced with pity at the flushed, beautiful face of her patient.

'He's sure to come soon. He's been released, according to the *Evening Standard*. What a sensation it's all been! And fancy that attractive-looking young woman who came to see No. 22 this morning putting herself out . . . '

'You never know what hell a human being is going through, do you?' remarked Sister cryptically.

Janine opened her glittering eyes.

'Peter,' she moaned. 'Oh, Peter . . . '

Then, suddenly, the nurse rose from her place beside No. 22. She saw another nurse coming down the ward with a tall, extremely handsome man whose lean brown face looked worn and weary and whose very blue eyes were exceedingly grim. She recognized him at once, because she had seen his photograph in several papers.

'It's Peter Willington,' she whispered to the Sister.

Peter came to Janine's bedside and the Sister beckoned to the probationer to put two screens around the important bed of No. 22.

Peter found himself sitting beside that narrow white bed, staring down at the girl he had loved and whom he believed he had married unlawfully.

Never had she looked more beautiful than with that bright pink flush of fever on her cheeks and the brilliant light in her green, Irish eyes. He looked at the thick fair plaits on either side the small head. Lovely and alluring even in the plain hospital nightgown and flannel jacket. He felt his heart contract. Somehow she looked so pitiful and so young. How could he be stern with her? And what right had he to judge?

'Janine,' he said, and bent over her and took one of her pretty hands in his.

The glazed eyes turned to him.

'Peter . . . Peter . . . ' moaned Janine.

He forgot all his bitterness. He was filled with compassion for her — an acute sense of tragedy, of sorrow pervaded him. He took her other hand and held the slim fingers in a close, strong grasp.

'I'm here, Jan,' he said. 'It's Peter here, speaking to you!'

She recognized him after a time. She gave a low cry.

'Peter, are you all right? Did she confess? Are you free?'

He bit his lip. A lump came into his throat. She might be bad — rotten — an adventuress — but her first thought was for him. Had she cared sincerely, after all?

'I'm all right,' he said. 'I'm free. Clare owned to it, poor soul. I'm free, Jan, and everything will be all right now.'

She gathered a little strength and

searched feverishly under her pillow for a piece of paper which she had steadfastly refused to part with since she regained consciousness. She gave it to Peter.

'You must read that. Nikko wrote it just before he died. Read it, Peter. You'll see I'm not quite so bad . . . as you think . . . '

Her voice trailed away weakly on a sob. She lay watching him, all her soul in her eyes, and he read what Nikko had to say.

The light of understanding sprang to Peter's eyes when he realized what those dying words meant. Jan had not committed bigamy. She had not betrayed him. She was still his wife.

Peter crumpled Nikko's confession in his hand. His lips were twitching and his emotion so intense in that moment that he could scarcely keep his control. He slipped on to one knee beside the bed and gathered Janine's slight figure into his arms. He held her with passionate tenderness and hid his face against her breast.

'Oh, my dear, my dear. I can hardly believe it. I've been a brute to you. I wouldn't believe you. Are you really my wife — mine — after all.'

She cried weakly against his heart.

'All yours and always have been. Peter, I've broken my heart for you. I love you so. Peter, Peter, don't leave me now.'

He cried.

'Never, never again. My darling, my darling, I'll never leave you again. But I've been such a swine to you — I didn't know — didn't understand — '

'How could you?' she whispered. 'But let's forget it and wipe it out — and begin again, dearest.'

'If you will,' he said. He looked down into her swimming eyes and his own were wet. 'If you will, my dear, my own. I've never ceased loving you, Jan, I just couldn't bear the idea that you belonged to *him*.'

'I didn't,' she panted. 'Never did. But I am absolutely yours. Peter — kiss me.

You haven't kissed me for such a long time.'

He held her closer.

'Sweetheart — you've been very ill. You must get better now . . . '

'Your kisses will cure me,' she whispered. The brightness of her eyes was not unnatural and feverish. They held the light of passion and love for the man who held her in his arms as though he could never let her go again.

Gradually, the ardent, lovely eyes closed. Peter touched her lips with his.

When the nurses came back they found Janine sleeping peacefully with her hand locked in the hands of her husband. And there was no longer any doubt in the minds of the Sister and her probationer that 'No. 22' would make a rapid and complete recovery.

Other titles in the Linford Romance Library:

ROMANTIC DOCTOR

Phyllis Mallett

1968: As a doctor at St Jermyn's Hospital, Ann Barling's work is her life, and it seems like romance has passed her by completely. She may as well admit to herself that she's now a confirmed spinster. When she returns to work after a holiday, however, change is afoot in the form of newly hired Dr David Hanbury. He has a reputation, and seems determined to add Ann to his list of conquests. But she's having none of it . . .

CHRISTMAS AT COORAH CREEK

Janet Gover

English nurse Katie Brooks is spending Christmas at Coorah Creek. She was certain that leaving London was the right decision, but her new job in the outback is more challenging than she ever imagined. Scott Collins rescued her on her first day and has been a source of comfort ever since. But he no longer calls the town home — it's too full of bad memories, and he doesn't plan on sticking around long. Scott needs to leave. Katie needs to stay. They have until Christms to decide their future . . .

THE CHRISTMAS CHOIR

Jo Bartlett

After a chance encounter with a young homeless man, high-flyer Anna reassesses her life. Handing in her notice at her City job, she returns home to St Nicholas Bay. There, she finds that the new vicar is none other than Jamie: the man who severed their relationship when they were teenagers, and took off abroad alone. The pair renew their old acquaintanceship — just as friends. But are the sparks of their long-ago love kindling into life once more?

JESSICA'S CHRISTMAS KISS

Alison May

When Jessica was fifteen, she shared a magical kiss with a mystery boy at a Christmas party. Now almost thirty, she is faced with a less than magical Christmas after uncovering her husband's secret affair. And, whilst she wouldn't admit it, she sometimes finds herself thinking about that perfect Christmas kiss, back when her life still seemed full of hope and possibility. But she never would have guessed that the boy she kissed in the kitchen all those years ago might still think about her too . . .